Crowe Press

ISBN: 978-1-939484-38-3

www.crowepress.com

www.martamoranbishop.com

The Between Times

Book Two – The Divide

Marta Moran Bishop

This book is dedicated to all the men and women, past and present, who have and will fight to promote equality and honor in our country, and to those who continue to fight for our freedom.

I want to thank my husband Ken for his continued support of my writing, often taking on more than his share of the household chores and losing me for hours at a time, as I sit at my computer.

A special thank you to my editor, Franki deMerle, who is and continues to be an inspiration to me.

The night holds sway over the world, and the dawn's light has not yet broken through the darkness. Night's mystery and silence fills the air with its magic.

Most of those souls who prefer the night to the day have put their heads upon their pillows, and those who are early risers are not yet up. The people who love the late nights and sleep till noon will eventually rise to the crash of sunlight.

I prefer to wake by letting the silence of the night hold me a little longer in its kingdom and allow the between times to gently guide me into the day, when the quietness of the earth and the tranquility of the stars are mine. For during the between times there is magic. Anything can happen, and the wall between the worlds is thin.

THE PROPHECY

For fifteen years, the prophecy spread by
word of mouth.

From mother to daughter, father to son, it
spread.

In the dark days of the United States of
America, a girl will be born. She will have
the power to make people fade from sight.
Sound will disappear with a wave of her
hand.

She will have the power to control the
between times, and during that time, the girl
child will call to her all the spirits of the
past, present, and future. They will come
and join hands with her. Together they will
become one power, one body, and that body
shall control the magic of the between times.

From that day forward, the darkness and despair will disappear from our country. The world will be made new, and all people will once again be equal under the eyes of the law. Kindness will return to our world. Men and women will no longer be the property of the rich.

Corporations will no longer have the power to dictate the lives of their employees, forcing them to remain stuck in a life of drudgery. Money will be made in abundance, but not at the expense of the lives of others. The American dream will return.

One

The petite girl's raven locks cascaded over her shoulders, covering her face and arms. Her golden brown fingers deftly wove the glamour into the cloth. By touch alone, her small, delicate hands sewed the light of the between times into the fabric.

When she wove, the small, dark room with its concrete floor disappeared, and Jewell forgot it. She became a part of the tapestry itself, losing herself and becoming one with it. The magical silver light wove itself in and out of the tapestry, as it channeled its way through her.

Little could be seen in the small basement room at this time of the day, which made it safe for her to open the curtain and let in the faint predawn light.

Perchance if someone did look in, all they would see is the dim red light of the smoldering coals in the stove waiting to be stoked.

Because of the prophecy, it was against the law to be awake and out of bed during the between times. Nonetheless, Jewell could only put the finishing touches into her tapestries at this time of day, for this dim light held a luminosity all its own. This heavenly light could not be understood, only felt. Even outside, little could be seen at this time of the day—only a fraction of the sky, if one looked up. The sun had not yet begun its journey over the horizon.

Jewell spent a portion of each day sitting at
her loom weaving.

Her tapestries came to life from somewhere
deep inside herself. The picture or design
was pulled from the very air into the cloth
without thought or purpose. The colors took
on a reality of their own. Each hue she
picked up in her slender fingers performed
its own task in the scene that unfolded. All
had their own destination in the overall
design. None seemed accidental; all had
their place.

If someone was watching, he might see a
glimmering silver light spill from the
window above her head. As it touched her
hair, a chorus of colors played through her
shimmering locks. From her head, the light
moved through her body to her fingers and

into the tapestry. This splendid light lit her from within.

As it flowed out of her fingers, it became the thread she used. It was the precise material that made up the universe. Its essence was virtually undetectable, unless you knew how to channel it. Her birth rite was the ability to sew the radiant silver light of the between times into cloth.

The bewitching, faint light worked its way into all of her tapestries. Each time, the blaze of the light added something unique to them. It gave them a beauty beyond words and more. That more could only be detected by Jewell and the wearer of the fabric, for each piece held magic of its own woven into the splendor of the cloth.

The small black cat threaded its way in and out of her legs. Almost like a familiar, it became a part of her, aiding her as it danced.

They became one being as they pulled in the power and glory that existed in the mystical universe and made it one with their souls.

"Sable, we have finished," Jewell said. "Father will be able to take two textiles to market with him tonight. I believe these are the most powerful and beautiful of all the pieces we have ever made," she told the little cat.

Sable jumped on her lap, and they sat for a moment. Jewell hummed a small tune, and the cat purred. Their voices harmonized together, and the song they made ushered in the dawn. Before she began each day, Jewell drew the curtain that she'd made out of one of her tapestries aside and let in the predawn light.

Sometimes she opened the window to let in a bit of fresh air. The air could not be called clean, as full of soot as it was, but at least it rid the small room of its dank, musky odors—the smells trapped in a closed room from cooking, coal burning, candles, and human bodies.

When the dawn lit the morning sky, she would close their one small window. That window gave her the only glimpse of life outside her room. Through it, she could see a tiny bit of the world that lay just outside their small, gloomy basement. There was not much to see, only a bit of sky covered with the clouds that raced each other across the sky. There were times she could make out a corner of the building, if she stretched her neck and peered out of the corner of the tiny window.

Most days she just enjoyed the slight breeze that moved through the room from the open window.

This brief time in the early morning, when she opened the window, became the only other time in her day when Jewell had contact with the outside world. Without that little window, she would have nothing but the one-half hour in the courtyard the law allowed her each day. She spent that period gathering water and washing their clothing. Not a minute remained to view the world around her.

With the growing light, Sable jumped from her lap, and Jewell stood and stretched. Her small frame shuddered from the chill that seeped through her body.

So long had she sat motionless that the cold of the concrete floor and the stone walls had gotten into her bones.

The day has begun, she thought, as she pulled the tapestry closed. *It is time to light the fire, get Father's breakfast, and pack his lunch.*

Even through the tapestry that covered their one small window, she could see the smoke and soot already filling the street. "I wonder how the moon and the light of dawn are able to find their way through the heavy haze. The ash from the factories and the soot from the coal stoves fills the air, till the sky is black as night," Jewell told Sable.

"It is father's short day at the factory, Sable. He gets so tired from working so many hours. I wish I could help him by working in the garden or going to the market."

I wonder if he considers Sunday short? She thought. *Even though he spends eight hours that day in the church, still, he is at home earlier.*

"I wonder what church is like, Sable. Did you know they do not allow women in church? Father told me, unlike the days when mother lived, they don't teach women to read or to think anymore. I wonder why these men that Father refers to; consider women too stupid to learn. He said these men consider women the spawn of evil and not worth redemption.

I do get so curious to know what the world is like outside of this room," She mused as she glanced out the window. Silence filled the room. The only sound came from the clank of metal as she stoked the fire. *Well, that is the last of our coal*, she thought, as she put the final dregs of their meager ration of coal into the fire. With a deft hand, she began to cut the bread for sandwiches and warm the soup.

Stumbling out of his sleeping alcove, Ben nodded at his daughter. His eyes were still half shut as he walked over to wash his face. Pouring a small amount of water into the bowl, he smiled as he smelled the tea Jewell had set on the small table next to his bowl of soup.

Jewell would not have served me tea today, unless she finished the other tapestry, he thought. Although tea was not as expensive as coffee, it was still costly, and here in the lower towns, it was only drunk on festive occasions. Usually, they drank only a tiny cup of water with their meals.

"I guess you finished the last cloth, Jewell," he stated just before the last spoonful of vegetable soup filled his mouth. Last night's leftovers made up his breakfast. *Sometimes their breakfast consisted of the leftovers from supper, and at other times the leftovers from breakfast became their supper. At least it wasn't oatmeal today. That would have meant fried oatmeal tonight,* Ben thought. *He had never been that fond of oatmeal, though he was exceedingly grateful for it. Oatmeal was a staple of life in the lower communities.*

"Yes Father, they are ready. You can take two of them with you today. I think they are the best I've ever made. The power was exceptionally strong this morning," she said, pointing at the tiny package that sat next to his lunch bag.

"There are two here, Jewell? Ben asked. I have never seen a package so small, daughter."

"These fold relatively small, Father, though they are rather large. Time is short, but I can take them out and show you, if you wish. Truly, they wove themselves."

"That's not necessary. I believe you, daughter, and I must not be late for work. All hell will break lose if I am. I could get demoted or worse yet, lose my job. I suppose I must keep my astonishment under control when I take them to show Jamie at the market."

Before Ben walked out the door of their room, he turned just once to look at his beautiful daughter. She stood in the middle of their shabby room.

The light from the coal stove threw a rainbow of highlights on to her thick, dark, wavy hair. Her skin, usually a golden, brown, looks a little darker in the dim light, he thought. "I'll be leaving now, and I'll see you tonight." He said.

He wished he had been able to give her more than the dark, cold room where she had spent most of her life. Rebecca had picked it out before she died. It held surprises. *Those secrets are capable of saving Jewell if necessary*, he thought. I must admit, *Jewell has done more than most people could have with the small cellar room and its concrete floors.*

Colorful tapestries covered the walls. On the floor lay the one handmade rug Rebecca and Ben had hidden there, before Rebecca was murdered. He knew Jewell spent many hours keeping everything as clean and as free of dust and soot as possible. Their one source of heat, the coal stove, also provided a place for them to cook, but it did cover the room in soot.

I expect it is quite a chore for her, Ben thought, as he began his journey to work.

Two

The burly man closed the door and began his long walk to the factory. The legs of his pants quickly became filthy up to his ankles with the black dust of the street. Dawn had broken. Ash filled sky, and the rising humidity brought the pollution from the factories lower to the ground. The visibility was barely a quarter of a mile, making it impossible for him to see past the middle of his own building.

The streets are quiet today, Ben thought.

Nothing could be seen, not even a cat or dog. Of course, everyone in the lower towns considered anything moving to be food. He did not know how Sable managed to stay alive in this world. Most of those he knew had not stooped to eating cockroaches, though he had heard that the sewer people ate them. He didn't know for sure. Many people, when kicked out of their community, did not live long enough to make it to the sewers, or so he had heard.

Once in a while, he caught a glimpse of one of the sewer people, but not often.

Ben always left for work early. It gave him a chance to think and visit with his friend, Carlos, but everything seemed empty of life this morning. He supposed it was the lack of visibility.

The buildings did not change between the communities, all of them short and long— two stories tall, a city block long, and each with multiple doorways, one door for each room. There were so many staircases running down the buildings, they appeared to be under construction all the time. Each staircase accommodated one doorway. There were no hallways in the buildings. The law did not allow people to have a place to meet out of sight of the magistrates or their minions.

Most of the buildings were built from red brick, though over the years, the ash and soot of the factories had turned them black. Wood was much too precious a commodity, to waste on the lower communities, so they were made of brick.

Each community had approximately two-hundred fifty people in it, give or take a few, depending upon the size of the families living there.

Ben did not consider it safe that the buildings contained so many people.

The courtyard held the community garden, and each man took his turn taking care of it. It provided a bit of extra food for their families and kept starvation at bay. As a result, it was extremely precious to the community. A twenty foot fence enclosed it. If the magistrate or corporation wanted to punish someone in the community, they locked the gate into the garden.

When the punishment ended and the guards opened the gate, often the men found that the weeds had strangled the vegetables. Sometimes the garden was dead. All the men in the community prayed they were never the cause of a locked gate. You could be sure that your neighbors would steal from the culprit's family, even if it meant someone dying.

Once, someone stole the milk out of a baby's mouth to feed their family, Ben thought, as he silently walked on.

Far off in the early dawn light, he looked at the upper town. There stood the remainder of the great city of Chicago. Seen from a distance, the buildings lit the sky like stars, the colors vying with each other.

The skyline always made him think of Emerald City, from the old movie, The Wizard of Oz. Tall walls surrounded the upper town, much too high for anyone from the lower town to sneak through, if they had wanted to. It was covered with a dome to keep the air quality pure. If the poor were caught in the upper town, it could mean their death, unless they had been sent for.

For what must have been the millionth time in the last twenty years, Ben thought about when the division began. *He knew when it happened. What he did not know was how people let it happen. Maybe they were as oblivious to everything that was not in their own narrow world as he was at the time.*

At one time, I lived in what is now the upper town, he thought.

I remember people complaining about how expensive food had become and how high the unemployment rate was. There were so many people out of work and no jobs. Every day we heard another story on the news, about people robbing, stealing, and killing one another.

In the newspapers, he read about men and women who committed suicide after killing their families. It seemed everywhere he looked dried blood had covered the streets. He didn't remember any revolution. However, he did remember reading about the dead and dying. People died of starvation, exposure, suicide, and of course the killings.

The judge ranted night after night at the dinner table about the new generation of politicians who cut out minimum wage, unemployment benefits, and social programs. He blamed the state of the country on them.

I should have listened more carefully, Ben thought. Rebecca did. *She listened attentively to my father. She questioned everything. The two of them discussed the possibility that it was all planned.*

Then they tried to find a purpose behind it. Each night their speculation grew. Mother and I usually remained silent. Neither of us wanted to believe it to be true.

I remember finding their conversation amusing. *I didn't believe it was possible that all these things they talked about could be happening. I am partly to blame*, Ben thought. *If I am honest with myself, it is probable that I am more to blame than most. Rebecca and the judge became extremely outspoken.*

In his courtroom, he began taking on the politicians and the corporations.

Unfortunately, each decision that he made against the corporations was brought before the appellate court, and all of them were overturned. Rebecca talked to groups of women and children. Both worked hard trying to show people how dangerous this slippery slope could become, Ben thought, gazing around.

On the day his parents died, his world changed. The police claimed it was a drive by shooting.

They said the disenfranchised poor killed his parents. Day after day he questioned the police about the investigation. Finally, they charged a group of men and gave them swift justice. At least, that is what the police and the Governor called it. However, these men had no trial. The police lined the men up along a wall and shot them.

Rebecca screamed the loudest. She did not believe these men had killed the judge. She believed it was a conspiracy. Maybe it was.

Ben didn't know. He did know that for the
next five years, even after Jewell's birth,
Rebecca continued to be especially
outspoken.

She railed against the new laws that
demeaned the poor women, making them no
more than breeding beasts.

He begged Rebecca to be silent. Each day,
some different horror became a part of their
new world. The Governor called out the
militia, and they built the wall that divided
the rich from the poor, the same wall that
stood today, dividing the communities and
separating the upper town from the lower.

The militia rounded up the poor and shut
them into the lower communities.
The U.S. Army Corps of Engineers gutted
the schools to make temporary rooms to

accommodate the poor. These rooms
became a model for the communities that
stood today.

All the single family homes in the lower
town were torn down because of 'bank
foreclosure,' even though many argued that
they paid their mortgage or they didn't have
a mortgage. Still they lost their homes, and
the new communities went up. Rich and
poor became separate societies. The
Governor said that with walls dividing them,
no longer could the poor of the city kill the
rich.

The walls would protect the rich. Rebecca
didn't care what the new laws were. She
slipped through the walls. Every day she
went down and taught the women and
children. The first time the guards caught
her, they slapped her on the wrist. The

second time the police caught her, it became more serious, and they warned her. The third time, they arrested her and levied a penalty on her family.

Still, Rebecca would not listen to Ben or her mother.

She continued to fight for the poor, just as Ben's father, the judge, had.

The fourth time they caught her in the lower towns, they took her away. Ben never saw her again until the day they killed her. After that, it was just him and Jewell. Rebecca had warned him,

"If it happens, Ben, let it be. Do not fight for me, Ben. Just take Jewell to the room in the lower town and hide. It will do no one any good to try to fight them." The corporations own the lower towns now.

Ben wondered about the rest of the country, but there was no way for him to find out. He did as Rebecca had instructed, took Jewell, and slipped into the lower town. The two of them had been there ever since.

He would never forget the day the magistrates had Rebecca brought back to the lower town, and right before his eyes, he watched Rebecca killed. *They burned her to death as a warning to all in the lower communities.*

The horror of that day became a reminder to all in the lower communities to mind their place. The memory never left him.

Three

Ben passed out of his community. He watched the small, thin man walk toward him.

Carlos' clothes are not much better than mine, Ben thought. *Maybe a bit more patched, but his wife has a deft hand with her stitching.*

"Hi Carlos," Ben said quietly. "My thoughts are on the communities today. Did you know that, in the old days, they referred to this type of building as an apartment complex? Now they call them communities, and each community is an island unto itself. It is sad, isn't it?" Changing the subject, he looked at his friend and said, "You know, I should have worn my mud boots today too."

"The dust is thick in the street today," Carlos said. "The street cleaners will have much to do today. Ben, I remember the house where I grew up. It was not far from here. I guess they tore it down to make way for a community.

There is one that stands in place of all of the houses that used to be on that street."
"Do you think there are any houses left in the lower towns, Carlos?" Ben asked.

"I haven't seen any, Ben. Each month since I was a boy, I have taken a different way home from church. Except, of course, for all the years I spent in the military," Carlos stated.

"You've never talked about those days, Carlos."

"No, I guess I try to block them out of my mind Ben. I was young when the world changed. The new laws said I must go into the military. You know how it is. When I got out at twenty-eight, they gave me a job and a wife for my service to the country.

I guess getting injured helped. I didn't need to remain in the army those last two years. I might not be here now if I had, what with all the wars."

"I never served, Carlos. I was thirty when that became law. I could hardly believe they would put a fifteen year old in the army though."

"The law I consider the worst is the one that will take my oldest boy away on his seventh birthday," Carlos added.

"He will go into apprenticeship until he is fifteen and then into the army. I will be lucky if I ever see him again. If I see him, will he even remember me? I wonder."
"I don't have a son Carlos, so I can only imagine your pain," Ben said.

"Ben, I know they will brainwash him. He will not even remember the things his mother and I taught him, and he will think of women as beasts for breeding children. It is what they teach the young ones now."
Carlos wiped his eyes. A tear threatened to run down his face.

Both men fell silent for a moment. "Carlos, I think women and girls have it worse, don't you?" he asked his friend.

"Yes, Ben. I think about my daughters and what will happen to them when they reach their majority. When you treat a woman like a beast, it breaks their spirit. The kind of man who will do this only sees the beauty of their youth and the work they can get out of them." Carlos was clearly distraught.

"I know what you mean, Carlos," Ben said very quietly. Few knew about Jewell. "I wonder the same about my daughter. How will I keep her safe from someone like my neighbor, Yusuf? He is a man who would use a woman until she dies, her body worn from childbirth and overwork. She will be sixteen in a few weeks. I am so afraid, Carlos."

"My friend, maybe the prophecy will happen, and it will protect her. If it doesn't, I do not know how any of us in the lower towns can protect our children. Even the servants who work for the rich in the upper town must follow the laws. Their children are subject to the same rules," Carlos said.

Ben agreed, "You are right, my friend. The servants may be treated a bit better, being one step above us in the hierarchy. The rich do not consider their servants to be people either. Only the rich and those who own the corporations are people. The rest of us have become less than human. I think it is a black time for our country.

As the path to the factory became crowded, Ben and Carlos walked on silently. They had stopped talking.

Many found them an odd pair—Carlos, thin, Hispanic, barely over five feet tall, and Ben, even though advanced in years, still had the build of a ball player. Ben was an immense man, dark skinned, tall, and broad shouldered.

Quietly they walked side by side. Now and then they glanced around at their world. Gone were the trees that used to line the streets. No squirrels or birds could be seen anywhere in the lower communities. There was only dust, black soot, and occasionally one could see blue peek through the clouds of smoke and smut that filled the sky.

To Ben, this world seemed dead. Nothing remained of beauty, in the lower towns for the youth to see what the world could be. Gone was the music that filled the streets and the flowers that grew in window boxes. Only in the morning and at the end of the work day did life stir on the streets in the lower towns.

Ben and Jewell lived in one of the poor
communities. Theirs was a mixed
community, because most of the folks who
lived in it were of mixed races.

Carlos and his family huddled in a two room
apartment in one of the Hispanic
communities. He had heard that the
conditions in the all-white communities
were a bit better, but not by much.

The men from different communities rarely
became friends. Sometimes during the few
minutes of break time allotted at work, the
lines between the communities broke, and
men talked to each other. Sometimes others,
like Carlos and Ben, met on the road,
walked to work together, and became
friends.

Most days, Ben and Carlos met each other on the path. Their communities were next to each other, so they had more time alone together. During the walk to work, they discussed the world or their families. Outside of their homes it was the only privacy the world afforded them.

They talked quietly, changing the subject if someone came within hearing. It served nothing to allow anyone to hear a private conversation. You never knew who the new snitches were.

The living conditions in all the communities were basically the same. Even so, jealousy and animosity sprung up between the communities. As a result, Ben and Carlos seldom spoke when other men joined them on the path to the factory. Since they lived in two different minority communities, just seeing them together was a cause for talk. If people knew they were staunch friends, it would make them especially suspect.

Each family, no matter the size, received up to two rooms. None of these rooms had running water or electricity. Only a few of the buildings still had plumbing and electrical wiring in them, but none of it had worked in years. Most of these were the older buildings that had been gutted to make the community rooms. All had some form of coal stove, which served for both cooking and heating.

Everyone that lived in the community got their water from the pump outside in the courtyard. Aside from the water that stood in the communal wash tub, each family received one large bucket of water a day. So strictly was the water rationed, people in the lower towns did not bathe frequently. More often than not, they cleaned themselves the best they could by reusing the same dirty rag, rarely even rewetting it. The rags became quite grimy.

I feel for Carlos, Ben thought. *His seven year old son would go to the apprentice hall this year. There, he would live with the rest of the apprentices until the age of fifteen. At fifteen, boys did their military duty until the age of thirty. If he lived, when he was thirty, he would go back to work for the corporation and possibly be allowed to marry.*

Marriage was something decided upon by the magistrates, and many times they only picked those men who were the community snitches.

At sixteen, the girls became women, and by law, they got married. Some of the women went to the snitches as payment for informing on other members in their community.

It was a hard life. Even snitches like Yusuf could lose favor easily enough. No one was safe.

Four

"Ben, I need you to stay a little late tonight. You don't mind, do you?" Mr. Horton asked with a smirk.

Keeping his head down, Ben did not make eye contact, for he did not want the man to see his reaction. He said quickly, "I'd be happy to, sir. I don't mind at all."

Out of the corner of his eye, Ben watched Mr. Horton slither. The man appeared smaller than he was because of his hunched back and thin frame.

Thank God he has moved off. I could barely keep from retching, Ben thought.

Mr. Horton's teeth were black with rot. The man positively reeked of stale beer, garlic, and unwashed clothes. Ben didn't think the man had washed or changed in months. The black, crusty rings around the man's neck and the cakes of dirt under his finger nails made Ben wonder if the man ever truly bathed.

Ben cringed at the thought of Mr. Horton touching him or even coming near.

At least Ben kept his teeth in decent shape, and even though his clothes were old, they were clean. So incrusted with dirt and grim, no one could tell anymore what color Mr. Horton's clothes were. Ben never believed fear management produced the best results, but it was now the way of the world.

With both hands scarred from years of hard labor, Ben moved quickly putting the lids on the jars of perfume destined for the upper town. Today they bottled perfume; tomorrow he might be using the welder again making bars for cages or water pipes.

Everything always goes to the upper town, Ben thought. *Seldom did anything go to the lower towns.*

"Does the factory seem darker than usual today, Carlos? Do you think they moved some of the lighting to one of the sections where they are making more delicate instruments?"

Standing next to Ben, Carlos, let out a sigh. "I think you are right. It does seem darker. I heard they began making a new type of weapon in one of the sections. They probably need the extra lighting over there."

"If that is true and rumors of that sort usually are, then that would definitely be the reason they moved the lighting." Ben said agreeing.

"I want you to know how sorry I am that the boss picked on you as an example tonight. I know it is your one early day. When he walked over, I feared it would be me again. Last night he had me here till nine o'clock. Then I only had two hours before curfew."

"I bet there was barely enough time to do the weeding in your community garden last night, Carlos."

"You're right, and I could not get to the market. My kids had to eat leftover fried oatmeal again. If I am lucky, I'll be able to pick up a bit at the market tonight, or it will be oatmeal all week. Five twelve-hour shifts and one fourteen have left me barely able to stand tonight.

Thank God we at least have that. My wife made an extra-large batch of oatmeal in case I can't get any coal tonight. It has gotten so low, if I can't pick any up, the oatmeal will not even be fried the rest of the week."

"Thank God we are all able to grow oats in the gardens, or on weeks like this, we would not have oatmeal to fall back on." Ben replied.

"You're so right. We must count our blessings I suppose."

"I know you feel the same, Carlos. The regular week is hard enough, but when you add in the extra four hours, that makes it nearly impossible." Carlos, even though small in stature, is strong and muscular, Ben thought. "It is hard on us all when the boss goes on his tirades. Somehow, I have to make it to the market tonight, and I have no choice, but I must weed the community garden tonight too."

"How will you manage that, Ben?" Carlos asked. "Is it truly possible to weed and shop in two hours? Curfew is at eleven o'clock. I'd be surprised if Mr. Horton doesn't keep you till nine o'clock, as he did to me last night. Can you get someone to trade with you, at the garden I mean? I know that is difficult. Most men aren't ready to give up a moment of their time off, even on a trade."

"No, I don't think there is anyone who will trade with me, Carlos. I know so few people who live in my community."

"I wish they would let us do a bit of weeding on Sunday, after church. Maybe they could have church run a bit less than eight hours."

"Shush, Carlos. You know if anyone other than me heard you say that, it would mean a fine. Too many are ready to squeal to get a bit extra from the magistrate."

"You are so right, Ben. Thanks for the reminder. I guess that would be considered blasphemy. I worry about you. Please don't get caught out after curfew, Ben."

"Still, somehow I must do it. I simply don't know how, Carlos, but I must.

There are things that cannot be put off or we do not eat at all this week, and we are nearly out of coal too. The coal rations barely get us through the month as it is, but you know what I mean."

"I know, Ben. The handful of extra coal we get, because of our three children, isn't enough, especially in the winter. Last winter the little one got terribly sick from the cold."

"I can hardly believe they expect a family of five to make it on only one extra handful of coal." Ben didn't mention Jewell. He never mentioned her at work.

Carlos understands how vital it is that everyone forgets about her, he thought. Unfortunately, it also means we only receive enough coal for one.

He knew Carlos would not bring up Jewell. Carlos knew Ben was trying to find a way to hide her from the magistrate before her sixteenth birthday. He didn't want the magistrate to marry her off to the highest bidder in a few weeks.

Too many already knew about her, like his neighbor, Yusuf. At least Yusuf had never seen her; though he had seen Rebecca in her day.

God, how I miss my Rebecca, Ben thought. *Jamie still lives in the upper town. Maybe, he will be able to help. I must remember to call him Soucy. There will be trouble if anyone finds out that we are friends. Nor can I let the snitches remember who my parents were or remember Rebecca, because if they remember Rebecca, they might begin thinking of Jewell, and I must protect her.* The closer it got to Jewell's sixteenth birthday, the more curious Ben became about the rest of the world. He'd take her out of the country if that was possible. He hoped Jamie would know. She had a bit of magic in her, and he feared for her. When she was of marriageable age, what would happen to her?

Speaking in hushed tones, Carlos said, "Ben, you are daydreaming again. You do not want to be caught doing that."

"Thanks. Carlos, I'm happy you are my friend. Faithful and true friends are rare these days. These twelve-hour shifts can be killers, especially when one is getting on in years like I am. When they make it a fourteen, I can barely hold up. I find it nearly unendurable."

"I just do not want you to get caught. The penalties are stiff. You heard what happened to old Jack, didn't you? I don't want that to happen to you. I like working next to you Ben. You are my friend," Carlos added.

"As you are mine, Carlos. Yes, I heard about old Jack. Have you seen him since they kicked him out of his community?"

"I saw him on the street; he moved pretty rapidly. I thought maybe I'd been seeing things at first, but it was Jack alright. I hear there is a city in the old sewer lines. The ones that lose their jobs and homes live down there."

"The ones they used to call the street people in the old days, Carlos?"

"Yes, you're right. I remember that. They did call them that once, didn't they? Except they can't live on the streets now, and they need to be extremely careful when they

come above ground. Jack used to be so
fastidious about his own personal
cleanliness. I could hardly believe it was
him. He smelled worse than Mr. Horton
does, but that probably comes from living in
the sewers. I would expect them to smell
putrid. There is no excuse for Mr. Horton. I
wonder where Mr. Horton got all the scars
on his face. Do you know, Ben?"

"I heard that his father beat him when he
was a boy. I met his father once. Be glad
you never met him. That was one real mean
man, Carlos. I heard tell he beat all his
children until they bled," Ben said.

"Seriously? That is atrocious, but I guess it
does explain why Mr. Horton is so awful. I
would think he would have learned some
sympathy, but apparently it does not work

that way. Didn't it used to be illegal to beat your kids?" Carlos asked.

"Chicago is not what it used to be, and Mr. Horton is a bit younger than you are, Carlos," Ben whispered.

"Is he truly? He looks ancient," Carlos replied.

"I guess it is from his old man, and the lack of personal hygiene," Ben answered. "I don't think his father allowed his children much in the way of food or water. Even before the rationing, water had become scarce. You remember, don't you, Carlos?"

"I was too young. I don't remember a lot about what it was like. I played ball with my friends, went to school, and helped with the work around the house. My father died in one of the gang shootings, before they put up the wall. After that the militia came and told us that we had half an hour to gather our things. They gave my mother and sister away in marriage. They took me to the military barracks. I heard my mother died soon after that." Carlos said with a catch in his throat. "I think they broke her spirit. Will you tell me one of your stories Ben? They give me hope for a better future," Carlos said quietly.

"Shush, Mr. Horton is coming this way." Ben put all his attention on the job. As Mr. Horton sauntered past them, all he saw was the two of them standing side by side. Both of them fell silent and concentrated entirely on their jobs, the giant black man and the thin, short, brown one. Looking at them with a smirk, Mr. Horton continued walking. He turned back now and then till he was out of sight, just to make sure they knew he had his eye on them.

"That was close, Ben. Mr. Horton scares me. He was the reason Jack ended up living in the sewers. I have a family to protect. I don't want my kids put into the state institute and my wife sold. She is not in her prime any longer, so it would be as a slave or servant for her.

I'm not like the rest of them, Ben. I love my wife and don't consider her to be just a breeding animal."

"You are a good man, Carlos. You remind me of my brother. He died a long time ago. I lost him in one of the wars. I don't remember if I told you he enlisted.

He believed the government, when it said we needed to go to war and he enlisted. I don't even remember now which war it was—there have been so many of them. Most of them are over religion, water, coal, and maybe oil now. I believe they still have oil and gasoline in the upper town, Carlos, but I don't know. Do you still want to hear about the old days?" Ben asked in a whisper. After a nod from Carlos, Ben began quietly to tell his story.

The two men did not look up from their machines, except to glance around to make sure no one was listening.

Five

"When I was a young man, there were no upper and lower towns in Chicago, Carlos. It was all one city. Even the poorest could visit the museums, if they had the money. Every child went to school, and loans were available for the poorer students to get a higher education. When young people turned eighteen, they registered to vote. Even the women voted," Ben said.

"Everyone voted and went to the museums and schools? How were they able to do this? I know my son will be seven soon, and begin his apprenticeship. I do not know how he'd find the time to go to school." Carlos' eyes were wide with disbelief.

"Corporations did not run the country then. There were small and large companies, and sometimes just mom and pop shops," Ben added. "It was not just the rich, the poor, and the sewer people. There were several layers of the middle class.

People didn't live in communities like ours, and they could choose where they shopped. There wasn't just a company store either.

"As a boy, I went to all the museums. A skeleton of a dinosaur stood in the Field Museum. It must have stood at least thirty feet tall. All the museums brought in exhibitions from all over the world. Why, my family all went to see the King Tut exhibit."

"Who is King Tut, Ben?" Carlos asked curiously.

"Thousands of years ago, in Egypt they called their kings, pharaohs. I don't know if there is still a country called Egypt. We get so little news anymore. Anyway, they buried their pharaohs with furniture, gold, and jewelry. Beautiful paintings adorned the walls of their tombs. Why, in some of the tombs there were receptacles that once held food and wine."

Carlos' eyes were wide in amazement, as he waited expectantly for Ben to continue. He wanted to hear another of Ben's stories about the old days in Chicago.

"All of the museums also had special rates for students and the elderly. In the Museum of Science and Industry, a doll house with electric lights took up a room all of its own. I swear it filled an entire room. That building was bigger than one of our communities.

"The Brookfield and Lincoln Park Zoos were full of exotic animals. Everything was open to the public. Of course, one had to pay admission, but it was open to everyone."

"Do you think those places are still there?" Carlos whispered.

"I cannot imagine the rich in the upper town not wanting to have the museums, the symphonies, and the zoos, Carlos. I know they were still there when I used to clean the streets in the upper town, before I came to work at the factory. I saw them," he answered.

Depression hit both men as they realized what their children had lost. Each man, buried in his own thoughts, standing side by side, fell silent.

I'm sure Carlos wishes his children could see these things just as much as I want Jewell to see them, Ben thought.

"Ben, do you think we will ever get those times back again?" Carlos whispered. "I mean do you believe the prophecy of the between times?"

"I haven't heard much about the prophecy, Carlos. Will you tell me?" He wanted to give his friend a chance to talk.

After looking around carefully, Carlos began, "It is said that a girl will be born who can control the magic of the between times. She will draw all the spirits from past, present and future together, and it will change the world. There will be no more upper and lower towns, and people will be equal again."

"How will she do that, Carlos? Does the prophecy say?" Ben asked curiously.

"The prophecy isn't too specific about the how. It just says that the magic she will create during the between times will unite the souls of all of those who were, are, and ever will be. The power that is created will be enough to change the world." Carlos' voice was full of awe.

Soon, the little man nodded at Ben, and left. His twelve-hour shift was over. He had four hours before curfew. It was enough to do a little shopping. Ben stood at his machine. Occasionally, Mr. Horton sauntered by, whip in hand ready to punish, if he found anything he could use against one of those doomed to work the extra hours that night.

Finally, just before nine o'clock, Mr. Horton walked by and gave Ben a nod to leave. He had kept him as long as the law allowed. Even Mr. Horton would not take a chance of making someone break curfew. It could be a death sentence for him. The law was particularly strict for those who lived in the lower towns.

Making his way as quickly as possible to the market, Ben wondered why Mr. Horton had decided to make an example of him that night. Carefully he looked around and let out a sigh of disgust at the evilness of people who were bullies. When they did it only to prove they could, it seemed especially malicious.

Those under them knew their lives depended on saying yes, even when it was not convenient—or worse, if the timing was awful, like tonight.

Six

The smell of unwashed bodies mixed with
beer, cigars, meat, perfume and spices, made
Ben want to throw up, as he pushed his way
through the crowded market. He hoped he
could catch Jamie's eye. If he could not do
it quickly, he'd only be able to stay long
enough to grab enough food to get him and
Jewell through the week, and of course, he
had to get their ration of coal.

He was still fuming over giving up his one
ten-hour shift. The boss knew that the men
used that day to shop and work in the
garden. They needed the one ten-hour shift
they got a week to do these things. The rest
of their shifts were twelve hours long—six
days of work, fifty-eight hours a week, if
they did not have to work overtime. The

worst of it was they received no bonus for working the extra four hours.

They were simply the ones used as an example. Nothing could be done on Sundays except church. That was the law. When a man had to work overtime and give up his one ten-hour shift, sometimes he had no food to feed his family. If only the law would allow women to help out with the shopping, but it didn't allow women out on the street. The law considered them to be breeding animals, without even the brains of a goat or a pig, and they weren't allowed to go to market. Ben knew better. Rebecca had held her own with any man and verbally bested many. By keeping the women at home and the men working fifty-eight hours a week, the corporations owned them all. *The corporations and the church made the laws. Rarely did a man have the time to rest or play with his children. How had it come to this? The United States was once the land of freedom*, Ben thought.

God, how he missed his Rebecca. With his priceless package carefully tucked under his coat, he made his way through the crowd. He tried not to get too close to anyone, or have the guards take notice of him as he slipped through the mob. His thoughts continued to play like a movie in his head.

When the boss asked you to work late, saying no was not an option. If you did, beware of the consequences. You might be reassigned to a lesser paying job, or worse, lose your job altogether and end up on the street. The company owned your hide, and they made no bones about it. Sometimes, they made an example of you, just to prove it.

Somehow, he would have to find a way to do his shopping and his work in the garden, or he would not be in the house before curfew. Mr. Horton would have notified the police to make sure they knew he stayed later than normal.

The walls have eyes, he thought, noticing yet another policeman out of the corner of his eye. *It was yet another way to keep them all on their toes.*

Why tonight? Mr. Horton knew it was the night he took care of his shopping and weeding the community garden. He only had the one day for it. God, he had never been at market so late. It seemed as if the worst of the lower community was here. He supposed it was because they wanted to get the best deal, and they knew that coming late assured them of that. He slipped in and out of the throngs of people.

Ah, there was Jamie's booth. Ben prayed; *let me catch his gaze quickly. He needed to trade Jewel's tapestries. He was sure he'd lose money on the trade tonight, even from his old friend, but there was no time to strike a reasonable bargain. Ben thought, I must get food for the week, and somehow figure out how to protect Jewell after her birthday next month. Where can I hide her?*

The history between Jamie and Ben dated back to the days before Chicago became two communities, when it was all one city, and everyone could venture into any part of it. Jamie and Ben went to the same school. Though Jamie was much younger than Ben, he worked hard. In school, Jamie was promoted many times, so they ended up in many of the same classes. Rebecca and Jamie were in the same age group, he was in many of her classes.

I'm lucky she chose me to marry—at least I had a few years with her, Ben thought.

Not many people, including those in the upper town, knew Jamie had a stall in the lower town. He kept a low profile in the lower community

After all it wouldn't help if anyone knew he owned one of the food corporations and lived in the upper town. Ben knew that he must call his friend "Soucy" when they met, it was not his real name, but he must remember, after all that was the name he used here.

Ben knew the things Jamie traded for here yielded extremely high prices in the upper town, especially Jewell's tapestries. But he comes here to see me too, Ben thought, as he caught his friend's eye.

Squeezing through the crowd around Soucy's stall, Ben watched. When Shyler took over, Soucy disappeared into the back of his booth. Ben quietly made his way around to the back and knocked on the door. Many candles and lanterns lit the room making it quite bright, Ben saw as he walked through the door into the interior. Quietly the two men hugged. It had been awhile since they had seen each other.

"What do you have for me tonight?" Jamie said softly. "Another tapestry or two I hope. I wish you would tell me where you get them. Someday you might not be around, but I'd still want to buy them."

Ben pulled out the package from under his coat. He laid two of the most beautiful tapestries Jewell had ever made on the table.

Jamie's eyes widened with marvel, and he let out a gasp before he caught himself. Having not seen either of the tapestries until now, Ben almost gasped himself. The tapestries were of the finest weave he had ever seen. They could be folded into a pouch the size of a man's wallet, and glistened with gold, silver, and all the colors of the rainbow on one side. The other side was incredibly difficult to describe, but the table it was lying on nearly disappeared in a haze of distorted light.

71

"You caught me old friend. I guess my bargaining won't fool you much tonight, will it, Ben? Besides being beautiful, what other unique qualities do these tapestries have, and what do you want for them?" Jamie asked.

"They do the usual things, my friend. Jumble sound so no one can hear you speak. Distort the vision so people do not see what you are doing, and one other thing. If you make these tapestries into clothing, people look the other way. It hides you from sight, unless you do something to draw attention to yourself. My time is short tonight, Jamie, so I will give you the fairest price I can.

"If we bargained, I would start at three thousand each, and you would start at one thousand each. We would end up around twenty-two hundred, maybe a bit more, since these are extremely beautiful, and you know it," Ben said.

"I wondered if you would even make it tonight, Ben. I was hoping we could sit, and have a chat like in the old days. It has been awhile. I guess if you can settle for eighteen hundred each, and a chat, we have a deal."

"If you want to visit awhile, our bargain will need to include a man to do my weeding tonight, groceries, and some coal. If not, then I'll be on my way, and come again next week," Ben said.

"We have a deal. I'll be back in just a moment, Ben. That way we can do a bit of catching up. Besides, I cannot afford what these are truly worth. So, if I throw a man in, we'll be even." He stepped out of the room.

As Ben waited he folded the tapestries. *Was there anything to the prophecy Carlos talked about,* he wondered. *He recalled Ana, Rebecca's mother, saying something about it before the turning. She even alluded that Jewell might be a part of it.*

Rebecca gave her life for Jewell, and the promise she made me make to keep her safe, Ben remembered.

He looked around the small room. It held an opulence rarely seen in the lower towns, though it would be considered poor in the upper town, he was sure. Jewell's tapestries hung from all four corners of the room, and incense burned, bringing the scent of wild roses to the room. It had been long since he had smelled anything as lovely. The incense he bought for Jewell in the market was never of this quality.

She would love some of this incense. Would Jamie sell him some, he wondered. *He needed to ask Jamie if he knew where he could hide Jewell and what he knew of the prophecy.*

"Do you remember Taft High School? We had such fun playing with the Eagles, didn't we, Ben?" Soucy said loudly. He walked in carrying a tray of tea. He thought how gratifying it would have been to offer his old friend a beer, but beer was against the law in the lower communities.

"How could I forget, Soucy? Those were fun days, weren't they? Undoubtedly, you were a brilliant tackle. I think you could have gone pro. Times change," Ben said as he pulled Jewell's tapestries across the doorway.

Finally, because of the magic of the tapestries, they could talk, and no one would hear them. Jamie continued. "I still do not understand why you stay in the lower town. I could work out a way for you to come back to the upper town, if you would let me. It has been a long time since Rebecca died. People have forgotten."

"I will reflect on that, Jamie. I am so afraid for Jewell, even in the upper town," Ben said mournfully.

"Ben, most of the older magistrates have retired now. In the upper town, the corporations no longer pay attention to you, if you keep your nose clean. The young ones honestly don't remember Rebecca. She is just a story they learned in school. It was nearly sixteen years ago, after all," he said quietly.

"Ben, the corporations have changed a bit, though not for the better. I reckon they remain concerned about the lower towns, and there is not as much attention to details in the upper town. They feel safe now, except for the prophecy of the between times. Things have loosened up in the upper town. The prophecy keeps the curfew in place for the lower communities. In the upper town, many people no longer believe there is such a thing as the between times. What with all the crowds and noise, most people no longer feel the magic, even if they are awake," he added.

"If you say so, but it still needs thinking on, Jamie. There are problems. Another friend mentioned the prophecy today. Can you tell me a bit more about it? We hear little in the lower towns."

"Ben, even in the upper town, the prophecy isn't talked about much. I think it is an example of putting your head in the sand. If someone mentions it, the room goes silent. There is still so much fear surrounding it. The magistrates and law makers call it a myth. At the corporation meetings, when they discuss the new laws, sometimes one of the younger members will bring the subject up. They would like to see some things loosened in the upper town. They wonder if the prophecy happened, would they lose their power. After all, the power is why their fathers worked so long and hard to change the laws."

"Jamie, are you telling me that our world changed so a few rich men could have more power?"

With a look of disgust, Jamie answered, "Unfortunately, that is what it is always about, Ben. Even the church has become all about power and control of the populace.

By taking away the ability of people to control their own lives and destinies, the corporations and those that own them make more money and have more power."

"That is horrid, Jamie. How did we get to this place? I remember our history lessons in high school. The founding fathers created The United States on solid principles. Everyone wanted to come here. It was the land of opportunity. I'm asking, because I was too busy playing football, and then I met Rebecca. I remember Rebecca and the judge ranting at the table about some things that were happening. I didn't listen when I

was home, not even to their speculations. I
don't know what happened.

One day I was playing football for the
Bears, and the next my world ended. The
world seemed to change quite abruptly
shortly after my father died."

Wistfully, Jamie looked at his friend. "Ben,
my father, Jeffreys, had your father
murdered. He tried to take on corporations
and politicians in his courtroom."

"What? They murdered my father?"

"Yes, Ben. I didn't tell you before, because I
did not find out until after my own father
died. It was then that I took over as C.E.O.
for the family corporation and began to sit
on the board. By then, Rebecca was dead,
and you had disappeared."

"How did it happen so quickly, Jamie?" Ben asked.

Seven

"Believe it or not, it was not quick, Ben. The process was an extremely slow, insidious one. It took years for these corporations to get their people into Congress and onto the judicial benches. First, they had to break the unions. The unions protected the workers, their wages, and working conditions. Unions had to be broken, so the corporations would have free rein to do and pay what they wanted. These unions held a lot of power. As long as they existed, they limited the corporations' power. Then of course, they needed to convince people that deregulating industries and banks would make everyone rich. These men bought elections for their handpicked men. With more of their chosen men in the Congress, they got more tax shelters, and other ways of hiding money became available."

"That was when the housing market collapsed, wasn't it?" Ben asked.

"Yes," Jamie replied. "They planned that too."

"It was what?"

"It was planned. By the housing market collapsing, many more homes could be bought up cheaply by the rich. Why do you think there are no homes in the lower towns?" Jamie said.

"Then science had to be debunked. It would not work if too many people believed that man was causing climate change. That is where religion came into play. They had a few men eager for their own power who continued to fight to have the theory of evolution thrown out in favor of the belief in creationism. They wouldn't even allow it to be a case of both being right and God's time was different than men's.

It became necessary for people to be divided into groups. It had to be them against us," Jamie went on. "Without the division they could not hope to divide and conquer. Nor could they hope to get the country into a position for a takeover."

"My Rebecca died because of greed?" Ben wanted to weep. Still, he kept his voice as low as possible. He needed answers.

"It was all greed and power, Ben." Jamie stated. "Still they needed more. They needed to control the population, especially women.

Women's brains think on a broader level. They look at cause and effect more than men do. The rich used religion to put women back in their boxes and took back the power over women's lives and the lives of their children."

"How did they manage to pull it off?" Ben said quietly, his head spinning.

"They used their power and religion to demean women, make them less relevant, and strip them of the right to control their bodies. This began with little things and grew. As the corporations controlled more and more of the Congress and the judges in the country, the little things became larger. It became acceptable for a lawmaker to state publicly that a woman could not get pregnant from rape or incest; women had magical juices to stop it."

"What? Magical juices? Come on, Jamie. That is hard to believe that someone, anyone, would say such a thing," Ben said.

"Sorry to disillusion you, but it is true. Some of them stated that if a woman became pregnant, then she had not really been raped.

She secretly wanted it. Statements like this were pure stupidity. They showed no understanding of science, biology, or critical thinking. They wanted it to be all a woman's fault."

"Jamie, how can anyone in their right mind truly consider rape to be a woman's fault?"

"Ben, that is an excellent question, and one I cannot answer. It is illogical and evil in my book."

"Then how could people believe such a thing, Jamie?"

"I don't know, Ben, but it got worse. A lawmaker in Wisconsin said that abused women should remember why they fell in love with their husbands.

They should take the beatings and go home to them. Lawmakers began bringing bills before the House of Representatives accusing single parents of being child abusers. This only served to keep women from leaving their husbands."

"You are kidding, aren't you, Jamie?"

"No, Ben, I am not, and yet it got worse. Congress began holding hearings on women's health issues, refusing to allow even fellow congresswomen into the meetings to advocate for women. It became a man's right to decide what a woman could or couldn't do with her body, or if she should be allowed medical treatment or insurance for certain types of cancers and other women's diseases."

"I can't believe it. How could they pull it off with only a handful of people?" Ben asked.

Jamie sat there looking as if he wanted to cry, and then answered. "They spent money and then more money. They used the money to plant people in areas where they could develop a seed of an idea. Next, they began to purchase elections. By outspending everyone with negative advertising, the voters stupidly elected the President the people in control wanted. The first thing he did was begin a religious war, so he could send men and boys to war. It was a diversion of sorts, and it worked. People in this country became frightened of anyone who looked or believed differently. The plan was to divide and conquer. It had worked during the Nazi regime as well as many others throughout history. The secret cabal of the rich knew it could work again.

"Distract, divide, take the races and sexes and turn them against each other. Take away jobs. Keep them afraid."

"Are you telling me that there was a master plan, Jamie?"

"Yes, Ben, and the thing I am most ashamed of is that my father, Jeffreys, played a significant role in it. If my father died fighting the evil as yours did, I would feel better. Instead, I have to live with the knowledge that he ruined so many lives, all in the name of greed. I hope you don't hate me, Ben."

"You are not responsible, Jamie," Ben answered. "I am glad though that you have learned so much. Tell on my friend, we still have a bit of time."

"The plan was multifold. Control all the branches of the government. Divide the races and sexes. Demean women and all who were not white, Christian men.

Then it was not enough to be a Christian— you had to belong to the right church too. Deregulate everything, so that a few could get rich enough to rule the world, because the government would not dare let them fail for fear the country would fall into bankruptcy or worse."

Ben sat there stunned. He still needed to know more, but time was growing short, and he needed to find out if Jamie could help him figure out how to hide Jewell. "Jamie, I need to get going in a few minutes, or I won't make curfew, but before I go, I need your help. In a few weeks, Jewell will be sixteen. I must find a way to hide her, or the magistrate will take her and marry her off to whoever is in favor. Can you help me prevent this?"

"I can help, Ben. I am going to give you a few things to take home. We will need to avoid meeting again for a while. It is essential for us not to be seen together too often.

Come back in two weeks. I'll try to see if I can pull some strings to get you out of work a little early that day. I need to think about how I can do that at the corporate level, without people tying us together.

"For now, let's just say I know of a place where Jewell can go. The prophecy is real, but for God's sake man; keep your mouth shut about it. There isn't time tonight to get into it all. In the meantime, educate Jewell with as much as you know. Hold on a minute," Jamie said, disappearing into the back room.

Sitting in stunned silence, sweat shimmering on his forehead, Ben waited. It wasn't long before Jamie rejoined him carrying four packages. One of them was exceptionally small, another was a bit bulkier, the third was obviously food, and the fourth was a ration of coal.

"This package contains your silver," Jamie said giving him the smallest package. Indicating the bulkier one, he continued, "Hide this one in your coat, Ben. It contains a few things for you and Jewell to study and something Jewell will need later. As you can see, these two have enough food for the week and a bit of coal. It will look better if it appears you did some shopping." Jamie handed him the last package. Ben turned toward the door, and Jamie stopped him. "One more thing, Ben," he said as he carefully placed a small bit of the wild rose incense in the food bag. "This is for Jewell. I saw you look at it and I know she would appreciate it."

Opening the door, Jamie said loudly, "See you later. It was fun to talk about your days playing football. Maybe we will see each other around again one day. Let me know if you decide to take me up on the job offer. Okay?"

"I will think about that, Soucy. Thanks again for the cup of tea and the chat," Ben said as he left with the silver pieces from the sale of the tapestries lining the small pocket in his coat. He had the package Jamie had given him for Jewell hidden in a secret compartment in the sleeve of his coat, and the bags containing the coal and food were tucked under his arm.

The market was empty. Most of the stalls were already closed as Ben made his way out onto the street.

I have about fifteen minutes to get home, Ben thought.

The guards would be watching carefully. He must not let them notice him.

After all, if they knew he had silver and he'd been able to get someone else to do his weeding, there would be hell to pay. Not to mention that having silver was illegal in the lower community. Whatever was in the package Jamie gave him was sure to be something that would make the guards want to question him further.

Eight

Quietly, the large man made his way home. He stayed in the shadows as much as possible. Head lowered, with his back a bit hunched to disguise himself, he continued to walk. Luckily, Jewell had sewn one of the older tapestries into the lining of his coat. It didn't exactly hide him, but it made the guards take less notice of him. If he was careful, it would keep him safe at least until after curfew.

The guards and police watched carefully for any movement on the streets after curfew. During those hours, no one was safe in the lower town except the magistrates, police, or the guards.

As he walked, Ben realized he could barely see the moon and stars through the thick layers of smog. It was late.

I shouldn't have dallied at the market so long, he thought. *Too many things could go wrong.*

If he didn't make it home before curfew, things could get mighty rough for him and Jewell. The best case scenario would be extra work. That would be hard, but acceptable. However, there was also the possibility that they would take Jewell away and turn her over to the magistrate or give her to someone in marriage—possibly even auction her off to the highest bidder. That would be intolerable. Of course, they might make the entire community suffer, and not allow them their community garden for the season. That would mean many people would go hungry. Hungry people made poor neighbors, especially if they believed it to be his fault. The others in the community might kick them out.

As poor as they were, they could suffer the fine, pull in their belts a little, Ben thought, hurrying down the dimly lit street. I must not look suspicious, or the guards might stop me just for shits and grins.

Deeper into the lower town he walked, nearly home now. Passing through each neighborhood, he noticed more similarities than he had this morning. Each building held one hundred units. The larger units were for the snitches and bosses in the factories, or they housed the families with multiple generations living together.

He and Jewell had a room in the basement at the middle of their building. He had planned it that way. That room had an escape hatch in the floor and a tunnel which led into the old sewer lines.

Ben felt the need to hurry before the first siren blasted. His mind was on the sirens as he walked. The first let everyone know curfew was nearly upon them. The second blast gave the five minute warning. By the time the final siren went off, you'd better already be indoors. People had been shot on sight—at least that was the rumor.

This used to be a beautiful city, Chicago, the windy city, Ben thought, looking back toward the shimmering lights of the upper town. The skyline looked like a magical city, if not Emerald City then maybe Rivendell from Lord of the Rings. He had seen both movies as a boy. People like Ben were no longer allowed to go into the city. Now movies were only for the rich.

As he swiftly walked home, he reminisced about his boyhood visits to the Art Museum, Museum of Science and Industry, and the Field Museum. He should describe them to Jewell soon.

She would enjoy the stories of the King Tut exhibit and the doll house. That was his last thought before the first siren screamed. It warned him the curfew was coming. He had just reached his door.

Ben knew Jewell would have hidden in the shadows, just in case someone was near him. She wouldn't show herself until he closed the door. She had listened to his warnings over the years. It wasn't safe for a woman to be seen, even a small girl child, at least not in this day and age.

After supper, they would talk a bit. She must be prepared. It was essential, not only for her survival, but if Rebecca had been right, she needed to be prepared for much more than that. It just might mean everyone's survival, he thought.

Nine

Her face was a mask of worry. Jewell smoothed her black cotton dress again. She glanced nervously around. "It's so dark in here, Sable. I do not know why Father told me not to put the candles on tonight," she whispered.

She lived her life in a whisper. Even Sable purred in a whisper.

"Father told me that before my birth, things were different. The lower communities were not separate from the upper town then. They were a part of a large, sprawling city, instead of a cluster of massive shanties on the outskirts of the factories that they are today.

Mind you, I have not seen these things," she said to the little cat. Just this dark room with its one small window high up near the ceiling, where I can just make out the light when it is a sunny day.

I haven't been anywhere except the back courtyard to get water to wash and cook with, and then only during my appointed times. In all my nearly sixteen years, I do not remember ever seeing anyone except you and father, Sable," she whispered.

"There are so many things I don't understand. Why did father tell me to set out supper early, if he would be late?" The small black cat continued to weave in and out of her legs, nearly tripping her as it wound itself into her long cotton gown.

Her small hands continued to twist the fabric as she paced. "I can't seem to sit still, Sable. I hope Father isn't bringing home a husband for me. I simply can't stand the thought of marrying someone I have never met or seen. I know it is the way of things, but it frightens me, Sable."

Her slippers barely made a sound as she walked over to make sure she had closed the tapestries covering the windows.

"It would not do if anyone were to look in and see you, Sable." Reaching down, she picked up the little black cat.

I don't know what I would have done all these years without you. How have you managed to stay clear of the butchers in this place? She put the little cat down on a chair and went quietly to the door to listen.

The walls are closing in on me tonight,
Jewell whispered. Please, don't let it all be
about a husband."

Sable mewed. Hush, little one. The walls
have ears. Oh please, let Father come
home."

Hearing a noise at the door, both Jewell and
Sable melted into the shadows.

Upon hearing the sound of voices outside,
Jewell pulled her shawl over her head to
hide her long black locks and backed further
into the darkness.

The cold seeped through the thin folds of her
dress, as she stood with her back pressed
hard against the rock wall.

Ten

"I could have sworn I heard a cat in your place just now, Benjamin. You know the rules. If you catch food in the building, it is to be shared."

"I have not seen a cat, Yusuf. Never have. Are you sure your hearing is alright? It is curfew, Yusuf. We must get in."

"I've been waiting for you. You sure are late tonight. Wanted to tell you, I have been feeling awful poorly lately. Maybe you will help me out tomorrow in the garden, Benjamin? You up to it?" Yusuf whined.

He was a vicious man with a pockmarked face, wide jowls, and a paunch around his middle. He always smelled like a privy, even outside, if you got downwind of him. The foulness of his clothes and breath were enough to make one lose one's supper.

I bet it would be horrid to be inside a room with this man, Ben thought. "Tomorrow will not be a good night, Yusuf. I had a hard day today, and I'm feeling my age a bit tonight.

Besides, I have another long day tomorrow. I think I will have dinner and hit the sack early the next couple of nights."

"So, Benjamin, isn't that little girl of yours near marrying age? You pick anyone yet?"

"Yusuf, mind your tongue or I'll mind it for you. She is none of your business, my friend."

"You don't have to get all high and mighty, Benjamin. Maybe I'll just have a visit with the magistrate and see what he has to say about my marrying your girl."

"Tell you what, Yusuf. Leave it be. We'll talk about that when she is a bit older. Maybe I can help you tomorrow, if I get inside, eat, and go to sleep right away tonight." Ben was trying to get away from this man. If he talked to him much longer, he was afraid he would swat him like a fly.

"Sure do appreciate your help, Benjamin, and as you say, we'll have that talk about your little girl soon. I bet she looks like her mother. I remember Rebecca before the burnings.

It was unfortunate that Rebecca remained a rebel and did not learn her place as a woman. She was a real looker—all that fair skin and long black hair."

One look at Benjamin's face and Yusuf decided to let go of that discussion for now.

"Don't forget tomorrow. There's a lot of weeding to do out there, if we are all going to eat this year." With a smirk, Yusuf lumbered off. He figured he had pushed just a wee bit too far, but it was fun to watch Benjamin squirm.

Ben waited near the door until Yusuf was far enough out of sight before putting his key into the lock. Quietly opening the door, he set his bags down and looked for Jewell. He knew she would be frightened. He opened his arms for her as soon as the door closed behind him.

Jewell, holding Sable, flung herself into his arms. Sable stopped purring and struggled to get away. She seldom liked to be held and hated to be squished between two people. Jewell's slender body shook as she clung to both Ben and the cat.

Smoothing her hair, Ben said quietly.

"Jewell let's eat. There are things I must tell you before bed. Time is short." Stepping out of his arms, Jewell put the small cat down on the floor, took the package from him, and made her way over to the small shelves near the stove. While she put the groceries on the shelf and the coal in the coal bin, Ben took off his work boots and stepped into his slippers. He hung his coat on the hook and washed the soot from his face and hands.

Sitting in front of the fire with plates on the small table between them, Ben began, "Mr. Horton made me work late tonight. After that, I stopped at the market and had a conversation with my friend, Jamie. He is younger than I am, but a nice man."

"I think I remember him, Father. I know you had weeding to do tonight too. Do you need me to come out early in the morning to help you? I know it is not legal for me to help, nor for us to be out in the between times, but maybe if we wear our cloaks and are extremely quiet, we can get away with it just this once."

Looking at his daughter with pride in his eyes, Ben told her, "Jamie sent a man over to do the weeding for me, so we could talk."

Sighing with relief, Jewell waited
expectantly for her father to tell her what
was on his mind.

She was nervous and hoped it wasn't about
her marriage.

Even if it was his friend Jamie, she didn't
feel ready.

"Jewell, eat. Your dinner is getting cold,"
Ben chided. "Tonight Jamie told me a lot
about how the world changed. He's going to
help find a place to hide you, so you will not
face marriage to someone like Yusuf."

"Will you come with me, Father?" she
asked.

"I don't know the particulars about that yet,"
he answered. "Still, I need to teach you

some things you will need to know. There are things you must know before you leave, in case I cannot be with you."

Getting up, he walked over to his coat and took the package Jamie had given him out of his pocket.

"Jamie sent this for you, Jewell. He said it might help explain things," Ben said, as he walked back to the fire and sat down.

Eleven

He watched as she opened the package. On top of a pile of black clothing lay a brown leather journal. The apparel consisted of a pair of black leather slippers, a black silk skirt divided at the legs making it appear to be pants, and a black silk blouse with a hood. Mystified, they both looked at the items she laid out on the table. "What are they for, Father?" she asked. Her fingers played across the softness of the fabric. "Such rich clothing—I cannot see what I would ever wear it for."

"I expect you will need this clothing when you are in hiding. Maybe you will need it on your trip to the place he is sending you," Ben said quietly.

"Father, I forgot to thank you for the incense. It is the most beautiful thing I have ever smelled. Though, I will have to use it in exceedingly small quantities so no one else smells it."

"The incense is a gift from Jamie, Jewell. He saw the look on my face and must have known I was thinking about how much you would like it,

Ben told his daughter with a smile on his face. Now back to business. Jamie said you must study the journal. He told me you would have need of each of the things he sent when the time came. Until then, you were to store them in a safe place.

Everything, except the journal, must not be used until the day comes for you to leave." By the tone of his voice, she knew she must listen extremely carefully. "Jewell, he also told me your grandmother is alive, and he will tell me more the next time we meet. In the meantime, read the journal, and we can talk about it over dinner this week."

"It's all so strange, Father, but you look dead tired. I'll not question you tonight."

"Thank you, daughter, I am extremely tired. I have much to tell you, but it will have to wait. I must get some sleep if I am to be of any use to either of us. Before I go to sleep, I want you to know I love you. I'm sorry I wasn't able to give you a better home, but there is a reason I picked this room.

I chose it to keep you safe. It has its secrets that I will tell you about later. Still, I wish I had been able to raise you in a bigger and prettier room."

"It is a pleasant enough room, Father. I can see the moon from our window, and I feel safe here. Sable has her ways to get in and out of this room. I think if we lived higher up in the building she would not be able to come and visit us. Jewell stood up, walked around the small, dark table and put her hand on his shoulder. I love you too, Father," she said with a quiver in her voice. He had never before told her that he loved her. She knew he did from all of the things he did for her, yet he had never before said it. Her eyes filled with tears from the many emotions that swelled in her heart.

Ben laid his hand over his daughter's and held it for a moment, before dragging himself out of the chair. *My God, I cannot believe how tired I am tonight*, he thought, as he moved to the left side of their small room, and pulled open a curtain.

Behind it, on the concrete floor laid a small
mattress with a candle beside it.

On the wall hung two hooks, one of them
held his Sunday-go-to-meeting clothes, and
the other held his clean work clothes. A
small, empty basket sat next to the hooks
waiting for his soiled clothing. On the left
side of the room, behind another curtain,
there was a small alcove. He lit the candle,
closed the curtain, and left Jewell standing
in front of the fire alone.

She continued to glance over at the pile of
black silk and the heavy brown journal lying
next to it, as she cleaned up the room. How
she ached to pick up the journal and begin
reading. Her father had taught her to read,
even though it was against the law for
women to learn to read. The sound of his
voice played over in her head, "I promised

your mother you would be educated. Please, do not ever share this information with anyone, Jewell. It could mean both of our deaths." She couldn't help but wonder why this was true. He had never been able to explain it to her.

Finally, she had the fire banked and the dishes cleared. She walked over to the table.

She carefully picked up the pile of black clothing and carried it to the opposite end of the room. Here, another tapestry hung, and behind it stood a little area identical to her father's. Her bed area had its own hidden alcove. Each alcove was very small and remarkably well concealed. They couldn't be seen unless you specifically looked for them. Each of them held a small trunk made of old plywood. The plywood was gray with age, and the brass hinges were quite green.

Nothing she had could clean them and restore them to their original brilliance. Her father had never told her where he had found the plywood, but in them, each hid their personal belongings—those things that were significant to them.

Ever so carefully, she removed a small paper container. Opening the paper, she looked at the picture her father had given her when she turned seven. It was a picture of her mother, Rebecca.

For a moment, she held it against her chest almost in a caress, before setting it aside.

She folded the clothes and placed them in the trunk on top of her stack of books. Then she placed the leather slippers, the journal, and the picture of her mother carefully on top of the clothing.

It was late. She thought, *tomorrow will be another day.*

What was in the journal, she wondered again. With Sable curled in her arms, she slept.

Twelve

When Ben rose the next day to get ready for work, Jewell was already up. *She always got up early,* he thought, admiring his daughter as she stood making a lunch for him to take to work. "You look just like your mother, Jewell," he said.

"Mother's skin was so much fairer than mine, Father. She was so beautiful. Do you truly think I look like her?" she asked shyly.

There were no mirrors in their room, so she had never seen herself. "I would like to look like you too, Father," she said quietly.

With pride in his voice, Ben answered, "Jewell, the slant of your eyes is just like mine.

Of course, your skin is also darker than your mothers too, and your hair is wavier than hers was.

Rebecca had the straightest, thickest hair I have ever seen. It appeared to have highlights of blue in the moonlight," he said wistfully.

"You miss her, don't you, Father?"

"Every day and every moment, I miss her. Now, I will be late again tonight, because I promised to help Yusuf weed.

His idea of help is to sit while someone else does his work, but there is nothing one can do about that.

Don't wait dinner for me; just leave a bit on the stove for me."

"That man scares me, Father. Just listening to his voice makes my blood run cold. I heard the two of you talking about me last night. I know you are only doing his work tonight to protect me. I wish it didn't have to be that way, but thank you, Father."

"There will always be men like Yusuf, Jewell.

I do look forward to getting it all finished and coming home though. Tomorrow is church.

At least I will have a day to rest up a bit. Everything will be okay, as long as I do not snore in church," Ben said cheerfully.

"I'll make sure I sit next to Carlos and his sons. Carlos will poke me if I start to nod off.

Then after church, we can talk over supper. We will both have much to say.

I am sure you will be able to share Jamie's journal with me, and I will tell you what he told me last night. Just knowing I don't have to work tomorrow will help me through today."

He said as he opened the door to leave.

Thirteen

Alone, Jewell sat at their tiny table staring around the room. Sable jumped on her lap, curled up, and purred quietly. "Where did you disappear to this morning? I wonder," she said to the little cat, as she stroked its silky fur. "I want so badly to go get the journal and open it, Sable, but I know I won't be able to put it down. So it must be chores first. Soon, it will be my turn at the wash tub in the courtyard. Can you hear that woman from upstairs? She is extremely noisy isn't she, Sable?

"I wonder if there are windows that look into the courtyard from the rooms above. I never thought about that before.

Maybe I am more cautious now, because I am almost at the age when women are given in marriage. It would be terrible to think someone like that Yusuf watched me when I washed our clothes.

Worse, he might see my face or a bit of my leg as I bend over." She hugged the little cat tightly. Horror was written all over her face at the thought of someone spying on her.

"Well let's get to it, little one. I have the sweeping to do." The rug became dirty quickly with the dirt dragged in from outdoors and the soot from the coal stove, but she loved the rug. It had been her mother's and the one thing her father had been able to save after the burnings.

"I wonder how he did it. I will have to ask him. There is so much I need to ask. Every time he answers one question, it seems a hundred more come into my mind before he gets home," she said in a whisper.

Before long, her black hair had fallen in a mess around her shoulders. Sweat streaked down her face and plastered her hair to her head.

"Lord, it is hot today. Even this far below ground, it is scorching. I am so glad we don't live in one of the upper rooms.

It must be unbearable. She said aloud.

"I don't know what I would do without you, Sable. Father would come home, and find me a bit mad if I didn't have you to talk to."

She tied her hair up on top her head for what felt like the thousandth time that day.

At last, the carpet and floors were all swept. Jewell turned to the little cat. Holding the door handle to the courtyard in one hand, their bucket and a few pieces of extra clothing in the other, she said, "Hide, little one. No one must see you. I fear if they did, it would be death for you."

Before she stepped out of the room, she peeked around the door. She needed to make sure everyone was gone.

Nervously she looked up at the windows thinking, *I don't know what is wrong with me today. It never occurred to me before that someone might watch.*

I guess it was the conversation I overheard last night.

Yusuf is such a slimy man. I feel as if I need to bathe after just hearing his voice.

The fence around the garden bathed the courtyard in shadows. A few gleams of sunlight clung to doorways and a small cherry tree stood off to the side in the community garden. Each person in the community cherished that tree. It gave them all a little beauty, and once a season, each family got a bit of sweet dessert.

The tall fence stood in the middle of the courtyard and surrounded the community garden. It offered shade and a measure of security. At least she knew no one could look out at her from the windows on the other side of the fence.

A little to the side stood the communal wash tub with its spigot to pump water. Jewell took her last bar of lye soap from the pocket of her dark brown cotton dress and laid it next to her on the rim of the wash tub.

For the first time, she noticed the rust on the rim of the tub. She wondered if it could be removed. If not, the community would need to find a way to purchase a new one or find something they could trade.

This one had been here as long as she could remember, sitting on the dirt in the courtyard. She guessed it was rusting from too many years and too many people washing.

There was never enough time to clean it properly either—not when each woman was only allotted one-half hour a day to wash and get water.

Quietly humming a little tune, she began her scrubbing. It was difficult to get the soot and grim out of her father's work clothes. Her hands were chaffed and red by the time she had finished from the cold water and harsh soap. Still, the clothes were clean. She wrung them dry and placed them on top of the bucket. She was so grateful that their bucket had a lid, or she didn't know how she would manage to get everything in and out in one trip. The law did not allow women to go back into the courtyard a second time, even if they forgot something.

If anything was left till her father came home, most likely someone would take it. Jewell thought.

Fourteen

Her hair falling out of its clips again, wet clothing in one hand and the bucket of fresh water in the other, Jewell entered the room. Gone was the little bit of early morning light that came through the window, leaving the small room in shadows once again. Still, there was enough light for her to see her way to the clothes line. The line hung behind the little curtain that contained the chemical toilet, a bowl and pitcher for washing up, and a hole in the floor to dump the dirty water.

Grateful once again to Jamie, she lit a small piece of the incense her father had brought home. Yesterday, she had used the last of her tiny stock that she hoarded. Her father bought her the incense each month with the money from the sale of her tapestries. She used it so that their clothes would smell nicer and not take on odors of the privy room.

She would rather have been able to hang them outside in the sunlight to dry, but she could never be sure they wouldn't be stolen before her father came home to retrieve them. Besides, with all the dirt and soot in the air, they would probably need washing again before they dried.

Finished with her chores, she took out a bone with a small bit of meat clinging to it and put it in their only pot to simmer. It would be soup again tonight, but at least they would have a tiny bit of meat to go with it. Supper would be a small affair that night. With her father getting home so late, she knew he wouldn't eat much. She didn't like

it when he ate such a small amount and
worked so hard, but she couldn't force him.
Finally, she had completed as much as she
possibly could, until the soup was ready for
the vegetables.

*The sun is sinking so low in the sky; soon I
will need to light a candle.* She thought. *The
room lost light so much earlier in the day
this time of year. One could believe it was
later than it was.* "Sable, I believe I will do
my weaving a bit later."

She walked over to the alcove, opened the
chest, and removed the journal. Her finger
tips smoothed the fine leather of the cover,
and they quivered with the desire to open it.
Carefully, she laid it on the table, got a small
cup of fresh water, sat down, and opened the
book. The moment she opened the book,
Sable jumped onto her lap. "Aha, Sable, you

are as curious as I am, aren't you, little one?" Jewell asked the little cat, and Sable mewed as if to answer.

Inside cover of the book, in spidery handwriting, was a letter to her.

Dear Jewell,

My name is Jamie, and your father's history with me goes back a long way. We've known each other since we were much younger than you are now. I have much I need to explain to you. Some things your father will be able to tell you. Some must come from me. I'm going to ask your forgiveness first. I hope you will find it in your heart to forgive me for the failings of my family. Although my family had much to do with the loss of

your mother and grandparents, as well as

your current living conditions, I was not

aware of these things until recently.

Still, I feel responsible for my family's

actions and believe it is my responsibility

to help solve the problems they had a hand

in creating.

Inside this journal, you will find details

of your family and the part mine played

in their deaths. I will tell your father

about the prophecy before I give him this

journal. He can fill you in on that and

why I believe you will be the one to bring

about its realization. You will also find a

map with instructions on how to reunite

with your grandmother, Ana. Yes, she is

still alive; she has been waiting for you.

While she waited, she built the society

that will help you to fulfill your destiny.

Your friend,

Jamie

Fifteen

The first page of the journal was a hand drawn map. The paths lead through the old sewer pipes that ran under the community buildings. The many twists and turns of the tunnels frightened Jewell just from looking at them. Still, she studied the map carefully. Places were marked on the map where the old sewer lines had collapsed, and it showed her a path up and out of the sewer. There were directions for which way to take on the street above, so she could again descend to the sewers. All places where the sewer people lived were also wisely marked.

After what seemed to be miles of sewer pipes, the map showed another cave-in. This one appeared different. Instead of climbing

to the street above, it led her into what
appeared to be an enormous cavern.
That cavern seemed to lead on for miles.
She had never been outside of their room,
except in the courtyard, and just studying the
twists and turns of the map scared her.

As promised, the book also contained the
story of her family. As she read, she
wondered how much her father knew about
it all.
March 5, 2020

I am putting down on paper my recollections
of the events surrounding the death of my
friend Benjamin's parents and his wife. I
first learned of how involved my father was
after he died. When my father, Jeffreys,
passed on, I became the Chief Executive
Officer of the family corporation.

Stuart, Ben's father, held the position of one of the most powerful judges in The United States of America. From the bench, he wielded a lot of power, and he used it wisely.

According to my father's papers, the judge began to see a pattern developing in the country, which favored any aspect of a corporation over personal freedom. My father and his cronies became frightened by the judge's knowledge. At first, they just watched him. Finally, it became obvious he would not keep the information to himself. He began to talk loudly to anyone who would listen. He talked to fellow judges, lawyers, and journalists who had not yet been bought off by the corporations. Worst of all, if a case came before him that involved the rights of an individual, particularly women and minorities; he settled it against the corporation nearly one hundred percent of the time.

This could not be tolerated. They planned a murder. These men knew it had to look as if it were the work of crazed individuals. By doing it this way, they could further erode the rights of the people.

The night it happened, Stuart and his wife, Lisa, were coming out of a restaurant after celebrating their fiftieth wedding anniversary. A car driving down the street slowed down. Shotguns were aimed out the windows, and bullets rained out onto the street. Both of your grandparents died along with three other innocent people, one of them a child only two years old.

Jewell, as much as I would like it to have been different, I must confess, my father was instrumental in setting up this murder.

When this happened, you were only a few
months old. Your mother Rebecca had
worked as Stuart's assistant. She was privy
to all of his work. She knew his mind as
well or better than Lisa did, having been a
lawyer herself. She began to notify the
media that this was a hit, not a random
killing.

But before she could prove anything,
someone broke into both Stuart's office and
home. The police said it looked like vandals,
and there was no proof left that showed
differently.

Still, she would not stop talking. This upset
the little cabal of men, whose plan it was to
take over the country. They used the new
laws demeaning women that had sprung up
around the country to bring Rebecca down.
These laws disallowed women many rights,

especially when it came to their health and the choice to marry or not marry. To further erode their hope that she might settle down and learn her new role as a wife and woman, Rebecca began to sneak into the lower towns to teach the women and children who lived there. This could not be tolerated. Women could not be allowed to learn to read, and the poor needed to be kept ignorant for the cabal's plans to work.

Women had to be subservient to men. My father and his friends decided to use Rebecca as an example of why women should not be allowed to vote or work. The decision was made to use Rebecca as a way to put all women on trial. By proclaiming that Rebecca was delusional, they proved that women did not have enough thought process to be trusted. The fourth time they caught her in the lower towns, they called her a traitor to the people. Still, she didn't back down. She fought.

Bloodshed began on the streets, as the men without jobs fought over food and women. They wanted to believe the lies the corporations fed them through the media. All their problems existed because women couldn't be trusted. Women held jobs that men should have. Women were the root of all evil. Brother killed brother. Religious leaders fanned the flames by claiming their fanatical branch was the one and only true belief.

The corporations won. They picked from the remaining religions and formed a state religion. The power and might of The United States military was used against those countries whose religions differed. It was another power grab by those few men

who ran some of the bigger corporations.
Again, they won.

As I watched your mother burning in the
first of the fires that destroyed our country,
leaving it as it is today, I vowed I would find
out how this happened and who the people
were who were involved in the plot.
Over the years, I lost track of your father. It
seemed everyone related to Rebecca had
disappeared. I watched and waited. I worked
to prove I was one of those who believed
totally in the rights of the rich over the poor.

Jewell, my heart is heavy, and I beg for your
forgiveness. My father was an
extraordinarily greedy and unscrupulous
man. He hated everyone and everything,
except money and power. During his
lifetime, the only thing that mattered to him
were those things he felt reflected his

superiority and allowed him to believe in his own importance. This included his family. Everyone he touched feared him. That is how my father and his friends destroyed The United States of America and your family. For this, I am sorrier than I can ever express.

The rest of this journal contains directions to reach your grandmother, Ana. She has built an underground city in the caverns beneath Chicago. They can be reached by traveling through the old sewer lines. In some places, there have been cave-ins. It is at these places that you might have to take to the street for a bit. I will have people in those areas to distract the police the night you travel.

Watch out for the sewer people. I have marked their living areas on the map. They are a bit mad from years of desperation and homelessness. There is a break in the last of the sewer lines that opens into the miles of caverns of which I speak. This is where your grandmother's community is.

Unfortunately, you must travel most of the way alone. Ben must stay behind to cover for you. I have not told him this. No one can know that you have left. They must not come looking for you. It is too close to the final days before the prophecy, and he must protect you and the people in the movement from discovery. My sister, Catherine, will meet you near the end of your journey and lead you the rest of the way. She will keep you safe until you reach your grandmother.

The clothes I have given you are made from a rare silk. I had one of your tapestries sewn into them, giving them a bit of power to hide you.

They are insulated to keep you warm in the cold tunnels and the slickness of the sewer walls will not stick to them.

Take care, Jewell. With luck, I will meet you on that final day, when you join all of us as one with the power of the between times.

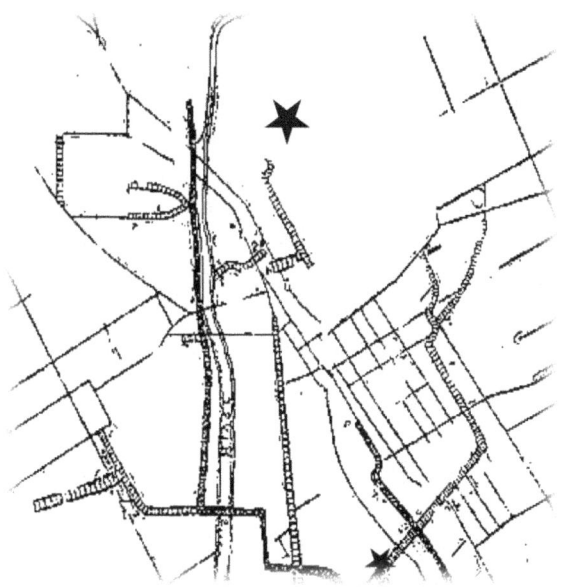

Sixteen

That night, for the very first time since she learned to weave, she had trouble. She just couldn't put herself in the correct frame of mind. Her thoughts continued to drift to all that Jamie had written in his journal.

She mourned for the loss of her mother, and she cried for her father and his losses. Her brain tried to comprehend many of the things she had never seen and ideas that had never crossed her mind. How glad she was that her father was going to be late that night. She needed a chance to absorb all she had learned, before he told her more. Besides, she didn't want to add to his burden by telling him she would have to go alone and leave him behind. Nor did she want him to see her cry.

Pacing the floor, unable to weave, she nearly
forgot to put the vegetables in the soup, until
the smell of the meat began filling the room.
She forced herself to stop her pacing and
took out their knife, removed the vegetables
from the bin near the shelving and
began cutting them. All the while she cut the
onions, carrots, and celery, she talked to
Sable. "What am I to do, Sable? How can I
learn overnight how to be brave? How can I
ever tell Father what I know?"

With vegetables simmering in the broth, she
picked up the black cat and sat petting it. For
once, outside of the few minutes they spent
during the between times after she finished
her weaving, the small cat sat on her lap and
allowed her to pet it.
Never before had she been so frightened.

151

She wasn't sure if she found it scarier to be forced into marriage to someone like Yusuf, or to leave this room and her father, and travel for miles in the old sewer lines. "I don't know if I can do it," she said again, jumping up. Sable landed on the floor. "Oh, Sable, I am sorry," she said, but although Sable would rub up against her legs, she would not allow Jewell to pick her up again.

She worried herself into a mess. She needed to get herself under control. It was late, and her father would be home soon. He had it hard enough.

He does not need to see me this way, she thought, as she deliberately and carefully placed the journal back into her trunk. Cautiously, she picked up the picture of Rebecca and hugged it to her. Then she gingerly touched her mother's face, smoothing the old photograph, attentive so she would not harm it.

Finally, feeling less rattled, she placed the photograph carefully back into the trunk and closed the lid.

She stirred the soup and took a small bowl off the shelf. She spooned a little soup into the bowl. "It will be cool enough for you to eat in a few minutes, Sable," she told the little cat. Usually Sable fended for herself. What she found to eat, Jewell did not know, but tonight Jewell desperately needed company, so she fed her friend.

Her father was still not home. It will be past curfew in a few minutes, she thought.

Suddenly she heard the sound of voices. It was him, and Yusuf was still with him.

Please, she prayed, make that man go away. Her prayers were answered a few minutes later. The door opened, and her father quietly came into the room.

He looks exhausted, even more tired than last night, she thought, rushing to take his coat and help him with his boots.

His warm hand covered hers for a moment. "I can tell whatever Jamie wrote in his journal has not set well with you, daughter. Am I right?" he asked.

"You are tired, Father. Let me get your supper ready while you wash up. After you have eaten, perhaps we will talk.

It is late though, and I feel better just knowing you are home. I think we should wait until tomorrow at dinner to discuss

Jamie and his journal.

I am okay, and it can wait," she said bravely,

and she felt her words to be the truth.

Seventeen

"You must not be seen coming or going. It could be the death of both of us, if the worst happens. Or I could lose my job, be flung out onto the streets, and you could be given to someone like Yusuf, because he is a snitch and in the magistrate's good graces."

Hands shaking, Jewell got to her feet without looking him in the eye, and asked, "Shall we have supper first, Father?"

Eating in silence, only of a bit of slurping could be heard now and then. Occasionally she pulled out a piece of the rabbit and set it on the floor for Sable, who sat quietly at their feet.

I do not know how Sable manages to know when I need her and shows up, Jewell thought. Nor did Jewell understand how the little black cat had been able to stay out of the eyes and ears of the rest of those living in the area, but she did. She had never been caught or sent to the butcher these many years. For that, Jewell was thankful.

Neither of them was happy, even though their meal was a banquet in comparison to their usual fare. It was real meat, not just tiny bits that once had clung to the bones her father bought at the market. It was their last meal together. Soon the hour would come when Jewell would need to enter the sewer lines. Neither of them knew if they would see the other again. Both of them worried for the other. Jewell worried, because she knew if someone found out she was missing, Ben could be put to death. Ben worried about his daughter walking through the dangerous tunnels alone. Neither ate much. They only picked at the food on their plates.

The only bright spots in the dark room were the tapestries Jewell had made. While looking at them, she asked, "If I leave now, Father, how will you manage? Who will get your supper, do your laundry, and supplement the money by making tapestries for you to sell?"

"Hush, Jewell. Don't mention your tapestries. Someone might hear. I wouldn't want someone like Yusuf to get wind that I had been selling on the black market.

The cloth you make brings a pretty price. Many of the rich have plenty to hide too. Especially the women, who like to keep their conversations private. The tapestries are one of the reasons I know your mother was right, and you are special," Ben said, gazing at the beautiful tapestry that covered their little window. Looking around the room at the tapestries covering all the walls, he continued, "Jewell, we would never have been able to even whisper in this room without your tapestries. You wove magic into them."

The two of them sat in silence for a moment as they looked about the cold, dark room. *She had tried to keep it clean*, Ben thought, *but without real light and with all the dirt the years have ground into this concrete floor, it was impossible. It wasn't like Rebecca used to keep their house before the burnings, but that had been a real house with floors, many windows, and rooms.*

Jewell's tapestries had given him the ability to teach her to read. His own sense of right and wrong made him give her a name and not refer to her as just "she" or "daughter," as the law stated.

The tapestries were magical; they blocked sound and the ability of others to see into the area. Because of them, we can see out and hear what is going on outside of this room, he mused.

"I must tell you about your mother now, Jewell. There is information you will need before you leave tomorrow, and our time is running short. Rebecca was and always will be the love of my life. She was beautiful, full of high spirits, laughter, and gaiety. She sang all the time, and her voice held the colors of the rainbow in it. Ana, her mother, was a strong-willed woman. She believed in equal rights for women, which is not a surprise, because that is how the world was when she grew up." Ben went on, "Chicago was a beautiful city then, with museums and music on street corners as well as at the theatre.

It wasn't only for the wealthy. It was for everyone, if they bought tickets. There were parks open to the public and gardens for all to visit for just a few pennies."

"It sounds incredible, Father." Jewell said dreamily.

Ben continued, "Best of all, women were considered people. They voted, worked, and went to school. They were doctors, lawyers, models, actresses, and anything else they chose. Ana and Rebecca told me a decade or so before the burnings that a woman almost became President of the United States. A few years later, the war on women began. First it was in small pockets across the country, but as the men who wanted power over us all began to gain more and more prominence across the land, it gained ground."

"Women voted and went to school, Father?" she asked with amazement in her voice.

"Yes, Jewell, they did," Ben answered. "Soon all the ills of our country began to be blamed on women's rights. The slogans became, 'America's downfall came when we gave women the right to vote.'

Men need to become men again and put women back in their place.' Corporations owned the media, and it became impossible to get real news.

We only got one sector's viewpoint. Everyone who dissented became hunted."

"Father, why was this allowed? Didn't people see what was happening? Why didn't women stand up for themselves? I don't understand," Jewell said, tears running down her cheeks as she thought about the heartache and loss of a way of life. "Things are so dark now. It seems so many are out to get whatever they can at the expense of others. Why can't women even talk with each other?"

"Jewell, please, don't cry. They put that law into place so that no woman could help another. No one could save another from a terrible situation. They could not help another woman to rise and fight to make things different. Your mother and grandmother continued to believe the country still had hope. They believed that someone would come along who would be able to use the between times to join women and men of like minds—someone who could bridge the gap between the past, present and the future to change our world. They believed it would be you.

That is why your grandmother hid when they came to take your mother. It is why your mother didn't fight the burning."

"Father, do you mean Jamie's letter was right, and my grandmother is still alive?" she whispered.

So quietly that Jewell had to lean toward him so her ear nearly touched his mouth, Ben said, "Yes."

"Why did they take Mother?"

Head in his hands, with tears running down both cheeks, Ben explained, "Rebecca was too outspoken. She refused to listen or live as a slave, locked in a room all day without the ability to see or speak to anyone but me. She knew the men in power would never allow her to raise you. Instead, they would take you away and lock you in the communal children's ward. They would not let you live with us. They did not trust what she would teach you."

Jewell's shawl fell off her head. Crying, she said, "Father, so many have lost so much by this way of life. Why was this necessary?"

Ben sat quietly for a minute, and then answered, "Jewell, your mother and grandmother believed it was a way to control us all. If we all lived in fear, each one against the other, scrambling to eat and keep a roof over our heads, we wouldn't be able to overturn the current status quo. We wouldn't know how to fight it. They take our women and children from us, if we don't appear to treat them like cattle. If we give them schooling or try to better our own education, we are ruined. It cannot be known that we read anything other than a few words of the 'Good Book.'

Alas, we gave them the power, and now we live in fear and darkness. They were right— your mother and grandmother."

Eighteen

"Be careful in the sewers, and when you reach the streets, don't get caught. It is a dangerous thing you do, leaving the house alone and after curfew."

"Will you tell me more about my mother, when I see you next, Father?"

"I believe your grandmother is with the women, daughter. She will tell you all you need to know. Please don't tell me where you are. If the guards catch on, they might torture me. I don't want to have an answer for them. Now go."

Creeping across the darkened room toward the trap door, Jewell again smoothed her dress. This time she ran her shaking fingers through her hair.

Then she pulled the black hood over her head and threw the shawl around her shoulders. She could barely see her father, as he stood in the middle of the room blocking the light from the fire. He seemed older tonight. Terrified, she put her first foot onto the rung of the ladder going into the cellar. She almost fell as Ben dropped a pan to the floor and yelled, "Now see what you have done." Over the noise her father made, nobody would hear the creak of her steps on the ladder.

Jewell jumped at every noise or movement as she crept through the tunnels. She was frightened. All her father told her was to go right at the end of the sewer line, follow the map, and keep walking. Jamie's letter said his sister; Catherine would find her and lead her to safety. She walked on with her father's words ringing in her ears.

"Remember, keep to the shadows. If you hear any noise, stop and melt into the dark corners.

There is danger—even in the old sewer lines. There will be places where they may have caved in, and you might have to climb to the street."

Silently, thankful for the slippers Jamie had given her, she slithered along the side of the sewer walls, grateful they were no longer in use. Weaving in and out of the shadows, she made her way to the end of the first set of pipes.

A large mound of earth lay in front of her. At some point in the past, there had been a cave-in. It was as her father said; she had to climb to the top and take to the streets until she passed this.

Even in the divided skirt, it was difficult to climb the mound. Her feet slipped, as the sand beneath them continued to give way. Finally, she reached the top and pulled herself up into the street. Off to the left was the sound of a man talking. Crouching in the dark, she paused.

It was one of the sheriffs. She held her breath and slid to the ground. Her slender hand covered her mouth to keep the sound of her breathing soft, and she waited. Another noise, a banging door, came from around the corner on the left.

Thank God the sheriff ran toward the noise. Soon, she could barely see his back. She ran through the small patch of light. Finally, she reached the corner. At the corner, she turned, and once again she moved into the shadows. Sneaking along close to the building, hiding in the dimness of the shadows, she prayed no one was in trouble, because she was confident that someone drew the guard away from her.

"Shush," a hand covered her mouth, and a woman pulled her into a doorway.

It was dark. Only a tiny bit of light was available for them to see where to put their next steps. "Follow me." The woman said as she led them to the ladder and they climbed down into the bowels of the earth again.

Below the city, there was a gloomy trail in front of them. "Shush," the woman said again, leading Jewell further down the faint path.

In this part of the sewer, the walls appeared to be full of a slimy muck, with bugs crawling all over them. They were even creepier than the first sewer lines and Jewell was afraid to touch them. These lines must still be in use, she thought.

The idea of getting too near the walls caked with filth frightened her as they walked on. They didn't speak, and she followed the woman. *She must be one of the women that Father said would find me*, Jewell thought.

Nineteen

Much further on, the tunnel got lower. The two women had to get on their knees and crawl for a while. There had been another cave-in, and the tunnels, though not quite collapsed were sagging heavily. Jewell suspected they were under the upper city now.

Finally, they saw an opening large enough for them to climb through, and then they entered the caverns. Unlike the sewers, the caverns were enormous, tall, and glorious. The rock gleamed with the many colors of granite, silver, and other minerals. In some places, Jewell could see stalagmites that seemed to rise like the pillars in the temple of the gods of ancient Egypt that she had read about. As they walked through another part of the cavern, stalactites hung from the ceiling, much as gigantic lanterns would hang. They were brilliant, these caverns.

Just ahead, it seemed to be getting brighter. The further they walked, the brighter the caverns grew, and more and more colors appeared in the rocks.

Soon, they were in a cavern so vast, it was difficult to see the end of it. There was a light brighter than any daylight Jewell had ever seen—even brighter than the sunlight was when she would go out for water in the courtyard. Maybe it was because the sky in the lower towns was always thick with a layer of smoke and fumes from the factories, Jewell thought.

The light hurt her eyes as they moved deeper into the huge area, forcing Jewell to put her hand up to cover them. The sound of women's voices, laughing, talking, and greeting each other could be heard.

One woman ran toward them. She held her arms wide, and with a smile on her face said, "Catherine, you made it. Thanks must be given to the mother."

"Mabel, this is Jewell, and she is Ana's granddaughter. It is said she might be the one."

Shyly, Jewell walked forward with them. Never before had she heard laughter, nor seen other women.

Heart in her hand, she walked into the center of the circle with Catherine and Mabel.

Catherine turned to her, a wide smile on her face, and greeted her. "Welcome Jewel, into the sisterhood." Catherine's golden hair appeared to be streaked with red in the glow of the light. Her face was wide and freckled. Her clothes were black like Jewell's and obviously expensive. Small diamond earrings sat in tiny holes in her earlobes.

She's so beautiful, Jewell thought.

Scanning each face, Jewell saw such variety it made her mind spin. There were faces with scars, some pockmarked, some brown, black, yellow—each race standing in front of her. All were smiling, all welcoming, all women, and a slow smile crept across her face.

It is odd, she thought. *I have not smiled often.* It felt strange for her face to do so.

Catherine took Jewell's hand and led her to a table laden with fruit, wine, bread, and cheese.

There was even a bit of meat. Jewell wondered how they managed to get this much food. She wondered how all these women came to be here. Mabel appeared extremely poor; her dress was frayed at the hemline. Some women had patches on their clothes, and others, like Catherine, looked like queens—so splendid were their clothes. There were so many questions she wanted to ask, but she was afraid.

Turning to her, Catherine said, "Jewell, I can see in your face that you wonder about my dress and why a woman, who is so obviously situated in a lofty place in society, would be down here taking such a chance. I will tell you some of it, and then after we eat, I will take you to the old mother."

"Catherine, why do the other women keep their distance from us?" Jewell asked, with a mouthful of food. All of Jewell's senses were working overtime. The taste buds in her mouth continued to be overwhelmed with each new bite she put in it. It was inconceivable to her how many women were singing.

The colors of the stalagmites made her lose her breath. And the laughter rang so loud, she wanted to laugh too.

"Jewel, they know you are shy, and they are giving you time to absorb it all, before bombarding you. Our movement grows every year. This year we have reached ten thousand in this community alone. Some of us, like me, are here part-time only or just visiting. We hope by next year, if we aren't living on the surface, we will double our numbers. There are many more such communities under this city and in other cities across the country. The old mother said we number in the millions now. Each year we grow. We wish we could attract more of the men folk, but they are afraid of losing their jobs or getting strung up on the blocks.

"Someday, the old mother tells us, the one who will lead us to the new world will be with us. All the signs point to it being you. Some of us believe it to be true."

"How can that be? Why me? I am nothing in this world. Why not you, Catherine? You have a higher status in society.

It seems you would have more influence,"
Jewell declared.

"It isn't influence we need. We need
someone who can draw on the magic of the
between times. So far, not one of us has
been able to comprehend what the old
mother means, when she states there is
magic to be used at that time of day. Try as
we might, and each of us does every minute
of every day, we can't seem to grasp the
piece that will help us understand it."

"What makes you think I can?" Jewell
asked. "Why do you risk so much? Who is
the old mother? How can the between times
help us?"

"Jewell, you have heard of the prophecy that
a raven haired girl will come along and draw
to her all the enchantment of the between

times. She will unite us as one and turn the world." Catherine seemed in a trance as she answered.

Looking around, Jewell realized that each woman in the room was silent, heads bowed as if in awe and prayer.

It felt almost as if they were kneeling.

Finally, someone laughed a bit hysterically, and the atmosphere in the room broke. Soon, all the women went back to their private conversations.

"I will take you to Ana now. She is your grandmother and the one we call the old mother. She will tell you some of our story, Jewel; she is the keeper of the history. Come along now."

Jewell followed Catherine across the enormous room and up to the door of the largest of the dwellings. "Wait here. I'll have to let you introduce yourself. I have much to catch up on and a small present to give to Cheryl for her new baby. I cannot stay tonight. It is too risky."

Catherine left Jewell standing alone waiting for Ana. Jewell glanced around the huge cavern.

There were candles everywhere. A massive fire stood in the middle of the enormous room, and a stream of fresh water cascaded down the side of one wall.

The water fell into a depression in the floor, making a clear pool of clean water. Around the huge fire was an entire city. There were rows upon rows of small, colorful, dwellings. The houses were built all the way to the back of the cavern.

Jewell wondered again where they were. If she were to climb to the streets above, would she find herself in the upper town, she wondered. *Am I still under Chicago?*

Twenty

A young girl with short red hair and green eyes opened the door before Jewell knocked. She ushered Jewell into the room. Shyly she said, "My name is Ellen. Ana is expecting you. Please, follow me."

Instead of being smaller than it looked on the outside, like the rooms in the lower town, this house was much larger. The front entry had long benches lining the walls and gigantic candlesticks standing on the floor. As Ellen led Jewell down a long hallway, she noticed the many doors that led to other rooms. At the end of the hallway, she and Jewell stopped, and Ellen knocked quietly.

From deep inside the room, an old voice spoke, "Bring her in, Ellen. I want to see my granddaughter."

Shaking with anticipation, Jewell followed Ellen into the room and stood in front of a woman who seemed ancient.

How could this old, white woman be my grandmother? Jewell thought.

"Ellen, would you please bring us some tea? Jewell, please, come sit here next to me where I can see you better," Ana said.

Jewell looked at her grandmother in awe. She tried to see a resemblance between the picture of her mother and the old woman, but found it difficult. She had a tough time even believing they were related. Ana's face was so old and wrinkled. Too much had happened in such a short time. Jewell was still reeling.

Finally, Ana said in a quiet tone, "You look just like your mother when she was your age. Rebecca would have been extremely proud of you."

Jewell looked into her grandmothers eyes, searching for the truth in her. Using all the knowledge she had learned from her father, she believed the old mother was telling the truth. With trepidation, she looked away, her gaze falling on each object in the room.

A piano stood near the wall with chairs lined up in front of it. She wondered if someone gave performances here.

"Jewell, I used to play when I was younger. Now, I give lessons to the young ones. My hands are too bent with age." Ana said, as she held her hands up and watched her granddaughter.

On top of the piano were many pictures. Jewell walked over and looked at each one. She recognized her father with a young woman she knew was her mother. How happy they looked together, she thought. Then she picked up a photograph of Rebecca holding a small baby with Ben standing next to her. It is my mother holding me. She thought with tears welling in her eyes.

Finally, Jewell realized she was being rude, but she still wasn't ready to talk to the old woman yet. She wasn't ready to be a part of this group of women, because she felt like an outsider.

Several tapestries covered the stone walls. The large room was a part of the cave. Perhaps, it was a hollowed out part of the cavern. She had read in an old history book that there were over one hundred and nine miles of manmade caverns under Chicago. She read that once people used these caverns for the rainwater runoff. She wondered if some of these caverns once had sewage flowing through them. The book she read wasn't clear about that.

She knew the sewage used to flow directly into Lake Michigan and the river, until scientists discovered how frightfully harmful it was to people.

On the other side of the room another open door stood. Opposite that room were more doors. One of them looked into a smaller room with a large bed on one side and a chest on the other. Another appeared to be a formal dining area, which held a table that would seat at least fifty people. Silver candlesticks were on the table, and over it a magnificent crystal chandelier hung.

The walls again were covered in massive tapestries, which would surely kept the cold out of the room.

She believed somewhere in this vast place must be the kitchen and sleeping rooms for other people. The opulence was something Jewell couldn't quite get her mind around.

Why, did she leave Father and me in the lower towns living in the one room in the basement, when she lived here, she wondered.

Everything she laid her eyes on made her think of more questions. So many questions filled her mind, she could contain her curiosity no longer. "Why did you never send for me before? Why did you leave Father and me alone to live in squalor and fear?"

"Jewell, sit down please." Ana said sternly. However, Jewell remained standing. "There is much to tell you, and I will explain everything. Yes, I will answer all of your questions.

First though, I will tell you about the promise your father and I made to your mother, Rebecca. She made both of us promise to allow you to stay with him to grow and develop in as much safety as he could give you.

She believed you had to experience what you would need to fight. If you never learned what it was like by living it, you couldn't comprehend it."

"I don't understand it, now," Jewell stated.

"I expect you don't, child. Rebecca gave her life to make sure all of us had a chance to change life as it is now. She knew what was happening. She could read the signs way before I did. In fact, I didn't believe her until the burnings started. That is my disgrace. However, she believed you would be the woman of the prophecy. She didn't believe you would be able to call on the magic of the between times, nor could you change things, if you didn't know what was wrong.

"She believed you had to understand it to the core of your being—not as a history lesson, but only as something you experienced.

Ben understood her and promised he would stay on the surface and make the best home he could for you. It was his job to make sure you were safe, while you grew and learned. He did it well too," Ana said quietly.

Jewell sank slowly into the chair. A glimmer of light filled her face as she realized the depth of sacrifice her mother and father had given for her to learn and understand.

"Ana," Jewell said, still not ready to call her Grandmother, "If the prophecy is about me, what do, I do? I know little about magic, or even about people. Why, I can barely converse with anyone. Until today, the only ones I have ever spoken to in my entire life are Father and Sable." The minute she spoke Sable's name, the little cat appeared, jumped on her lap, and purred. Astonished, Jewell nonetheless stroked the little cat.

"Granddaughter, knowing people and how to communicate verbally with them is a learned skill, one you learn just as you learned how to pull the power of the between times into yourself.

Just like you learned how to channel it through you and change the cloth you wove. Your tapestries might be meant to delight the eye, but they are so much more, aren't they?"

"Yes," Jewell whispered. "They do magical things, but I don't have any idea what makes them work.

I don't understand what happens when I weave, or how Sable and I use the between times."

"You are a channel. In a few hours, the between times will be upon us, and then you and I will see if you can channel the magic through us both. Until then, a bit of food and a little rest is in store for both of us."

"Ellen," Ana called, as she clapped her hands. "It is time. Please, set the table. Come, Jewell. Yes, my dear, Sable is welcome to join us too."

Twenty-One

Jewell helped her grandmother down the long hallway to the kitchen. Sable followed along behind them. She didn't dance between Jewell's legs as she usually did. She probably realized even with the cane Ana was unsteady on her feet.

As they walked, Ana pointed out the different rooms they passed. They turned a corner and Ana stopped. On either side of the hallway were two doors. "This one will be your sleeping room while you are here," she said, opening the door on the right. "The one across the hallway is the privy. I am sure you will want to wash your hands and face before we eat."

"Yes, I would, Grandmother," Jewell said.

"Then let us hurry to the kitchen, and once I am seated, you can come back here and wash. How does that sound?"

"That would be wonderful," Jewell answered.

Soon they arrived in the kitchen. Ellen was laying out bowls for the stew she had cooked earlier.
After helping Ana get settled into her chair, she excused herself. Scurrying back down the hallway, Jewell quickly reached the privy. Opening the door, she expected to see a room much the same as their privy in the lower town. Instead, a large porcelain tub with claw feet sat at the far end of the room. On the other wall were the commode and a porcelain sink. With a flip of a handle, the water poured out into the sink, filling the bowl with lovely warm water.

After washing, she walked back to the kitchen and arrived in time to enjoy the stew Ellen had made. Even Sable had a bowl of her own sitting near Jewell's chair. The room was quiet, except for the sounds of Sable lapping her stew and the women eating.

Before she had finished, Jewell found herself nodding off. Embarrassed as she yawned again, she apologized, "I am so sorry. I don't mean to be rude."

"Jewell, you must be exhausted. We have to be up in a few hours. Why don't we both get a nap?" her grandmother suggested.

As tired as she had been, Jewell awoke, just as she always did, when night still held the world before the between times. She never slept through them and believed she never would.

Getting quickly up from the bed, she walked into the bathroom, splashed water on her face, and made her way to the large room her grandmother had shown her last night. The room had no ceiling; flowers covered the walls, and a canopy of trees became its ceiling. In the middle of the garden room, sitting on a bench was her grandmother.

"Come over here, child. The between time is almost upon us. I knew you would need to try this first with just us. I didn't believe you would want your first time to be with ten thousand others. Was I right?"

"Yes, Grandmother," Jewell said.

Ana smiled; she noticed the use of the word "grandmother." Her heart warmed with love.

"It is coming, Grandmother. Take my hand now," Jewell said quickly. Just as they joined hands, the sky lightened; the sun was not yet over the horizon.

They were in the between time. As the luminance hit Jewell it sank into to her, lighting her up from within. It traveled down the length of her arm into her hand and traveled through her hand into Ana.

As it moved through Ana, the two women became one force. Both Ana and Jewell lost themselves in the magic of the between times. Jewell gathered up the light inside her and allowed it to flow outward, filling the entire room with the glistening movement of a shimmering light. It appeared to pull power from the very trees and plants in the garden.

All too soon, the power died. As it fled it left both women filled with hope and abundance.

Twenty-Two

Dawn broke the spell, lighting the garden with radiance and filling each leaf and flower, leaving no dark corners. They sat there on the bench watching the sunlight glimmer on the plants.

Neither was ready to talk or even look at each other. Their bodies were still lit with a radiant beauty.

They didn't even notice Sable sitting between them on the bench—so enchanted they were.

Even the spell of the between times couldn't last forever. Finally, the two women looked at each other and smiled as they heard the sound of footsteps coming into the garden.

Soon the room filled. At least a hundred women stood silently until finally, Mabel said, "We could feel it all the way through the entire village. It does work, doesn't it? She is the chosen one."

Embarrassed, Jewell let her dark hair fall over her face as she lowered her head.

Ana raised hers high and smiled. "Yes, she is. In three days it will be her sixteenth birthday, and the blue moon will fill the sky.

It will also be the day of the prophecy. Send the word out into the world to be ready. Gather everyone possible. Now go get word to all those who cannot come here to be ready at the appointed hour. We must have all who are of like minds ready to join us."

"Old mother, how will it work?" Mabel
asked. "How can those who cannot grasp
hands with us in this cavern, join?"

"Have faith, dear Mabel. It will happen. The
energy and power is extremely strong. With
the joining of those of us who are here in
this cavern, we will reach out and gather
those who are not here. We will pull all the
spirits together."

Ana held herself with a majesty seldom seen
before by any of them.

"For now, go send out the messengers, eat,
sleep and make ready. We must be prepared.

There may be at least two hundred thousand
people. They will need to share our space
for a day or two.

We have much to do! Please, send one or two of the women over to help Ellen make this house ready to receive guests too."

"Two hundred thousand people, you say?" Mabel said looking around at the faces of the women who stood near her. Not one of them could believe that even this enormous cavern could hold so many people.

"Yes, I believe we will have that many here physically. Mentally there will be more.

Why, even the dining room in the big house must be made ready with beds. We will fill each nook and cranny with people.

These people must be fed too. Now off with you all. Jewell will need a bit of food and sleep.

There is much to do and little time," Ana said with such authority as to make all the women turn as one and move out of the garden.

Twenty-Three

Jewell walked through the cavern and saw that each corner was filled with beds. Every family had removed all the furniture and odds and ends that could be spared from their homes. There was a bustle the likes of which Jewell had never seen before. Even her father's stories of football games and museums didn't come close to the level of activity around her.

Every now and then, a small child or one of the women would reach out and touch her. Gently and with reverence, not to scare her or get into her space, but to pull from her a sense of trust and belief that it would work. All of them wanted to believe it would work. They needed to believe in the magic.

Each and every person in this vast cavern hoped, including all those who filled the miles of caverns that stretched under Chicago.

All of them had loved ones in both the upper and lower towns. Yes, even in the upper towns there were those who wanted a better world. Men like Ben's friend, Jamie, and his sister, Catherine, could lose their lives if the authorities discovered they were a part of this movement.

Jewell hated the adulation. It made her cringe until she wanted to hide. She started to wear her cloak during her walks. It gave her a certain amount of privacy and helped conceal her. Ana told her to rest; however, she had always been active. She didn't even have sweeping or weaving to keep her occupied. So she walked and watched.

The morning of the second day, she saw her father. He was with a group of men, women and children being ushered into the cavern. She ran to him, not realizing that with her cloak on even he couldn't see her.

Quickly pulling it off her head, she threw her slender arms around him. Tears of happiness covered her face.

She had not realized how worried she had been about him. As they stood together, arms linked, silence filled the entire cavern. Both father and daughter pulled away laughing.

"Jewell, this is my friend, Jamie. You have met his sister, Catherine." Turning to his other side, he said, "These are my friend Carlos and his family."

Shyly, she nodded at them all. A shock of pure electricity went through her as her eyes met Jamie's. "Where are you all staying?" she asked.

"We are not sure yet, Jewell, no one has told us. We do hope it doesn't become necessary to separate us though," Ben said to his daughter, looking around at the group of his friends. All of them nodded in agreement.

"Let me check, Father, but I am sure that there is room at Ana's. If there is not enough room, we will make enough for you all. It is going to be crowded everywhere. I want us to be together. Come with me, please," she said as she walked off.

Jamie, Catherine, Carlos, and his family followed Jewell and Ben through the cavern to the large dwelling in the back. "Wait here," she said after leaving them in the foyer.

Soon she came back with Ellen, and the two of them led the group deeper into the house. Ben and Jamie would share a room.

Carlos and his family would have another room and Catherine would bunk with Ellen. That left the entire house, except for the dining room, filled to capacity. Both Jewell and Ellen knew that too would be filled before nightfall.

They all held on to the hope that the world would be changed before dawn tomorrow. Many had no place to go back to if it didn't. Jamie had left his boardroom, closed his home and disappeared. Carlos and Ben would not have jobs to go back to, and as a result, wouldn't have rooms for them or their families either.

Jamie and his sister might be able to go back to the upper town, if no one noticed they had gone missing. Ben and Carlos had not gone to work, so they would lose their jobs. Jewell was sure it had already been discovered that they had taken their families and disappeared.

At least half of the people in that enormous cavern feared the outcome. All of them prayed that the magic would work.

Twenty-Four

Jewell felt the burden of responsibility keenly. What if she couldn't do it? What would happen to all these people who depended upon her? There was not enough room for them all to stay in the caverns permanently. Where would they go? What would become of them all?

Curled up on the bed, Sable lying next to her, Jewell dozed. Unable to sleep, yet too tired to stay awake, she tossed and turned. Sable purred and patted her face each time she woke.

"Can I do it, Sable?" Jewell asked the little cat over and over again.

Sable only purred and curled up closer to comfort Jewell.

She woke to a rap on the door. It was a quiet sound. Still it nearly made her jump out of her skin. Flinging the door open, she saw Ellen standing there. "Your grandmother wants to see you, ma'am."

"Okay, please tell my grandmother I will be right there." Ellen left the room.

After a quick rinse of her face and a brush through her thick, dark hair, Jewell walked to her grandmother's room. All this noise must be taking its toll on the old woman, she thought, as she lightly knocked on the door.

"Come in, child," she heard as she opened the door.

"You wanted to see me, Grandmother?" Jewell asked.

"Sit down dear," Ana said. "I know how scared you must be feeling right now. I bet you are thinking that the fate of each person here is on your shoulders, aren't you?"

All she could say was, "Yes." It seemed not another sound would come out of her mouth. She began quivering so badly that Ana thought her granddaughter might faint.

"Jewell, come here and sit down, please."

Putting her arm around the trembling girl, Ana began to hum to her. Soon the humming became a little song—a song Jewell remembered from when she was a baby.

"Did my mother sing that song to me?" Jewell asked.

"Yes, she did. I wondered if you would remember," Ana said. "You were so young. I didn't think you would remember. Now that you have calmed down a little, I am going help you. At least, I hope it will help.

When I first fled the upper world after your mother died, I found myself in nearly the same position as you are. All of the people who are here were praying I could save them. They needed me to give them something to live for and a home. I know your fear is much worse than mine, and you are right to be afraid. It is true if we fail, then we are all doomed."

"I know, Grandmother. What I don't know is if I can do it. I know it worked with the two of us. I don't know if I can hold on to the power and channel it through so many people.

Then according to the prophecy, we must pull in all those who have died, including my mother, as well as those who are in other secret cities across the country. I don't know if I have that in me. What if I can't?"

"Jewell, I don't know either. What I do know is we must try or allow ourselves to be doomed.

If it doesn't work or if we don't try, we will be doomed."

Her face wet with tears Jewell asked, "Why?"

"Because, dear, children will still be born and grow up in a world of drudgery. The boys would have to go to work at age seven and then to war. The girls would become the property of a man and die young from either a beating or from having too many babies.

Many babies would die without a chance, and everyone would still be living a life of drudgery and near slavery owned by the corporation.

Their families would be threatened at every turn. We must try, darling."

"I'm so scared," Jewell said.

"We all are. It isn't just you; it is all of us. We all must believe, have faith, and allow the energy of the between times to fill us. It is not only up to you, dear. Each of us must help," Ana said.

Clinging to her grandmother, the first woman she had touched in over fifteen years, the girl gained strength.

"Now, Jewell, get something to eat. I will too. Go to your room, bathe and sleep. We have a lot to do in a few hours."

"Thank you, Grandmother," she said as she walked out of the room.

After following the long hallway, she stopped at her father's door and tapped lightly. "Father, I just wanted to let you know I will do my best," she said as Ben came to the door.

He put his arms around her, rested his head on hers and whispered. "You will do wonderfully, daughter."

Twenty-Five

Jewell and Ana sat on the bench in the garden room and waited. Slowly the room filled. Each person stood so close to one another that they could feel the breath of the person next to them.

The hour crept nearer. Each looked at one another and took the hand next to them. All had hope on their faces and tears in their eyes, as the predawn light began filling the room with the magic of the between times.

Sable sat on Jewell's lap. Ana's hand held her granddaughter's, and Jewell put her other hand out into the air. The glimmering glow of the enchanted moment filled the air. Silver bells could be heard chiming as the power of all those in the room joined together. The predawn light hit Jewell's hand, ran through her body, and filled it. It ran down her hand into Ana's and passed through Ana. From Ana it flowed outward through the person who held Ana's hand into the crowd of people, and on it went, out into the crowd.

It filled each person in the cavern.

Each person's soul became empowered. Their faces glowed with an inner light as it filled them. The light raced through the crowd, and yet a piece of the light was still in Jewell's right hand. As the crowd watched the magic of the moment, they saw something they would never forget to their dying day. They would tell their children's children. Those watching saw a shadowy hand appear and grasp Jewell's right hand. The sound of tinkling bells and magical light filled the room. The very air held the images of women, children, men—all those who had gone before them.

Rebecca held Jewell's right hand and Ana her left. Jewell looked out into the crowd, meeting the teary eyes of her father. The circle completed itself just as dawn broke.

The Beginning?

WHAT'S REAL AND NOT REAL

The attempted coup in 1933 to overthrow the government of the United States of America and President Franklin D. Roosevelt by a group of millionaires failed. The author used some of the congressional records, along with accounts from the book by Jules Archer, 'The Plot to Seize The White House: The Shocking True Story of the Conspiracy to Overthrow FDR,' to reconstruct fictional scenarios of what might have happened during this period. Some of the people involved can be found in documents in the Library of Congress, while others are purely fictional.

In the 1930s, the du Pont and Morgan family empires dominated the American corporate elite, and their representatives were central figures in organizing and funding the American Liberty League. The du Pont family was so complicit in this fascist organization that James Farley, FDR's postmaster general and one of his closest advisors, said the American Liberty League "ought to be called the American Cellophane League" because "first it's a DuPont product and second, you can see right through it'" (Donald R. McCoy, Coming of Age). Gerard Colby, in his book DuPont Dynasty, outlines the family's pivotal role in creating and funding the League. The Dickstein-McCormack Committee learned that weapons and equipment for the fascist plotters' Croix de feu-like super army "could be obtained from the Remington Arms Co., on credit through the DuPonts." DuPont had acquired control of the arms company in 1932.

Irénée du Pont (1876-1963)
By Charles Higham

Irénée, the most imposing and influential member of the du Pont clan, was obsessed with Hitler's principles. He keenly followed the future Fuhrer's career in the 1920s. On Sept. 7, 1926, in a speech to the American Chemical Society, he advocated a race of supermen, to be achieved by injecting particular drugs into them in boyhood to make their characters to order. He insisted his men reach physical standards, equivalent to that of a Marine and have blood as pure as that in the veins of the Vikings. Even though he had Jewish blood in his running through his veins, his anti-Semitism matched that of Hitler.

In outright defiance of Roosevelt's desire to improve working conditions for the average man, GM and the Du Ponts instituted the speedup systems. These forced men to work at terrifying speeds on the assembly lines. Many died of the heat and pressure, increased by fear of losing their jobs. Irénée paid almost $1 million from his pocket for armed and gas-equipped stormtroopers, modeled on the Gestapo, to sweep through the plants and beat up anyone who proved rebellious. He hired the Pinkerton Agency to send its swarms of detectives through the whole [du Pont] chemicals, munitions and auto-empire to spy on left-wingers or other malcontents.

The formation of the American Liberty League, "to combat radicalism" and "defend and uphold the Constitution," was announced shortly afterward. Heading and directing this organization were men from the du Pont and J.P. Morgan companies.

In 1934, several other pro-fascist organizations became active to combat the New Deal and the policies of FDR, but the most prominent was the recently formed America Liberty League. It was founded and supported by the Morgan's, the du Ponts, and the Pews, the Harriman's, the Mellon's, Remington, the Rockefellers, and other wealthy industrialists, per the 1947 investigation into Un-American Activities.

The American Liberty League propaganda said social security would "mark the end of democracy."

Although du Pont and J.P. Morgan companies were founders of the American Liberties League, no actual testimony that has been made public incriminating them or members of their family in the real conspiracy.

Harry Koch, the grandfather of Charles and David Koch, did own The Quanah Tribune in Texas. The paper did do propaganda for the American Liberty League.

William (Herman) Moran was head of the Secret Service through five Presidencies, and the great, great-granduncle of the author.

Howard Moran was a prominent banker at the time, as well as Herman Moran's brother. He did pay off his clients with his fortune. He was the great, great grandfather of the author.

In 1958, the John Birch society was created. Its primary purpose was to limit government. Harry Lynde Bradley, the co-founder of the Allen Bradley Company and the Lynde and Harry Bradley Foundation, Fred C. Koch, founder of Koch Industries, Robert Waring Stoddard, President of Wyman-Gordon, a major industrial enterprise, were among the founding members. Another was Revilo P. Oliver, a University of Illinois professor. The society is still in existence today.

The Tenther movement is real, and its design is to bring more sovereignty back to the states and limit Federal government involvement, including Fair Labor Laws, Child Labor Laws and Employee Safety Laws.

The Freedom Caucus, formerly called the Tea Baggers, and The Tea Party were all founded on the previous movements, and the Koch Brothers were one of the original backers of the movement. Just as the Koch brother's grandfather helped spread the propaganda of the America Liberty League, back in the 1930's,

Charles and David Koch helped fund the Tea Bagger a.k.a. Tea Party a.k.a. Freedom Caucus movement.

A man was elected to office who is and has put into place a cabinet designed to do away with all regulations, including those for clean air and water. Education for the poor and middle class is under assault, as are Social Security and Medicare. Women's health, affordable health care for all but the wealthiest among us, voting rights, and the rights of the minorities.

The press and the rule of law are under attack today.

This book is a work of fiction, the names, places, and people are all fictional, except for those that are from public records.

Other books by Marta Moran Bishop are:

Wee Three: A Mother's Love in Verse

Innocence and Wonder

A Poet's Journey: Sunlight and Shadows

A Poet's Journey: Emotions

Dinky: The Nurse Mare's Foal

And the short paranormal story

The Void

You can find Marta Moran Bishop at

www.martamoranbishop.com

www.martambishop@blogspot.com

On twitter @moranbishop and on Facebook

at **http://tinyurl.com/cu22fsa**

Sources: http://www.politicususa.com/proof-
war-women.html

http://bldgblog.blogspot.com/2010/09/artificial-
caverns-expanding-beneath.html

http://www.encyclopedia.chicagohistory.org/pages
/367.html

https://en.wikipedia.org/wiki/William_H._Moran

https://en.wikipedia.org/wiki/John_Birch_Society

Gerard Colby, Du Pont Dynasty, 1984

Trading with the Enemy: An Expose of the Nazi-
American Money Plot 1933-1949, 1983.

http://coat.ncf.ca/our_magazine/links/53/dupont.
html

http://coat.ncf.ca/our_magazine/links/53/spivak-
NewMasses.pdf

http://kochtruths.blogspot.com/2014_04_01_archi
ve.html

http://coat.ncf.ca/our_magazine/links/53/Plot1.ht
ml

https://www.americanprogress.org/issues/civil-liberties/report/2010/07/19/8033/doomed-to-repeat-history/

https://en.wikipedia.org/wiki/Tenther_movement

http://www.wanttoknow.info/plottoseizethewhitehouse

The Plot to Seize The White House by Jules Archer

https://www.amazon.com/dp/B00VKI49X0/ref=dp-kindle-redirect?_encoding=UTF8&btkr=1

The Divide

Book One – Darkness Descends

Book Two – The Between Times